11/96

Photocopies

JOHN BERGER

Photocopies

Pantheon Books New York

Copyright © 1996 by John Berger

All rights reserved under International and Pan-American
Copyright Conventions. Published in the United States by
Pantheon Books, a division of Random House, Inc., New York,
and distributed in Canada by Random House of Canada
Limited, Toronto. Originally published in Germany in a shorter
version by Carl Hanser Verlag in 1995 as *Mann und Frau,
unter einem Pflaumenbaum stehend*. This edition originally published
in Great Britain by Bloomsbury Publishing Plc, London.

Library of Congress Cataloging-in-Publication Data
Berger, John.
Photocopies / John Berger.
p.   cm.
ISBN 0-679-43525-5
I. Title.
PR6052.E564P48   1996
823'.914—dc 20   96-11650   CIP

Random House Web Address: http://www.randomhouse.com

Printed in the United States of America

First American Edition

2   4   6   8   9   7   5   3   1

For
WOLFRAM SCHÜTTE
at the Frankfurter Rundschau
who was the godfather and first editor
of these Photocopies

[Contents]

Photocopies

PHOTO BY MARISA CAMINO

[1]

A Woman and Man
Standing by a Plum Tree

At seven in the evening a yellow car pulled up by the house. The yellow of a French post van. But the car had Spanish plates. On its bonnet were stuck pieces of Scotch tape. Painted yellow. Not quite the same yellow. The car, however, was parked where nobody had ever parked a car. It was a possible place. It didn't obstruct there. But nobody had seen the place before.

The driver wore jeans and a dusty black shirt with white buttons. She had come from Galicia.

I had seen her once previously in my life. For five minutes in Madrid. I was giving a public reading there, and, afterwards, this woman, about thirty years old, came and handed me a roll of brown paper. It is a present for you. I unrolled it and saw a drawing. She earned her living, she said, restoring frescos in churches. When something is covered in plaster and you put it under water, the white is washed off, and its usual colour comes back. But often when it dries again, it looks a little whitish. It can even happen to your fingernails. When the woman said she restored frescos, I thought I saw a little of this whitishness on her clothes, on the backs of her hands. Before I could ask her anything more, she had disappeared.

Later I looked at her drawing. It had something to do with the world of fishes. I wanted to thank her, but I hadn't caught her name and the signature on the drawing was hard to decipher. The first name began with M and the second, I thought, with C.

Now this unknown restorer of frescos had arrived unexpectedly. I discovered her name. We talked of this and that: of Galicia, peasants, Paul Klee, the Documenta exhibition in Kessel. It seems we talked of nothing. If she came, it wasn't really to talk.

She came like one of her drawings about the world of fishes, or perhaps about the world of animals. She lives with animals. Certain animals. She knows their secrets, which are not secrets to them, but secrets from us. I doubt whether she chose the animals she lives with; they, I guess, chose her. Which would be normal, for it is they who live in her. Inhabit her. They were sitting invisibly inside her at the table.

She lives with them as she lives with her own kidneys, her own oesophagus, her own gall bladder. If she were dissected on an operating table, her animals would no longer be there – just as when the timber of a forest is felled, the wood-cutters never find boars or foxes or woodpeckers.

They come and go, her animals, and she's aware of each departure, and each new arrival. They produce irritations, they provoke impulses and, especially, they show her tricks, theirs. The tricks perform themselves in her, under her skin. This is what

4

I thought as we looked at each other across the table.

What animals? If she was asked, *they* would never let her reply. All animals except man are cautious. So they would never allow a catalogue. And she respects their animal caution. She even imitates it – I could see this as I watched her fingers.

She sat there drinking her coffee in her black shirt. Her hair was freshly washed, but probably she had not been to a coiffeur for years. In another life but with the same physical presence, she might have looked after (or stolen) horses – a figure disappearing on the edge of a wood, riding one horse and leading another. She was thin and sinewy like those who live close to horses. But in her present life she made mysterious drawings on home-made paper, she restored frescos and the animals who were closest to her were no longer of the Equidae family.

This time it was perhaps the Mustelidae family. The *belette* with her black tail, or the ermine, sharp, timid, who leads where you've never been! Animals who live, not play, hide-and-seek, and who can bite two ears at the same time, because so swift, whose bellies are white and prized by judges, and who have learnt from the snake to undulate their bodies as they accelerate, dip, curve, disappear.

We ate supper. Outside it started to rain, hard. We insisted she stayed the night. I showed her where she could wash and sleep. She stopped before a drawing framed on the wall in the kitchen and gazed at it. She didn't look intently. She just gazed at this drawing of figures with some writing around them. The writing was a quotation from the Eumenides about the Furies demanding vengeance, and another from the Gospel of St John: '. . . my peace I give unto you: not as the world giveth, give I unto you. Let not your heart be troubled, neither let it be afraid.'

She didn't say anything or make any sign. Her face was turned away. Simply her body announced how she was familiar with these words. Her body made no movement. No gesture. Just a withdrawal which might be mistaken for insolence.

All that night it rained.

The next morning she said she must be on her way to Kessel. Before she left, could she take a photograph?

We were drinking coffee in the kitchen.

You saw my camera? she asked.

No.

You didn't notice it last night?

She nodded to where her haversack was, on the floor near the door. Beside her haversack was a box which I had indeed noticed because of its silver colour. About the size of a mechanic's tool box. In places it had been repaired with black sealing tape. I hadn't asked myself what she carried in it. Maybe paints. Or apples. Or sandals and sun-tan lotion.

Like the original camera, she said, like the first! And she handed me the box. It weighed nothing. Its sides were made of plywood.

There's not enough light here, she said, let's go outside.

We went out to the plum trees where there's a table in the grass and there she looked up at the still cloudy sky. Between two minutes and three, she calculated out loud, and placed the box carefully on the edge of the table. In the centre of one of its long sides there was a white rectangular plaster, like you put over a small blister or burn. This plaster was framed by black tape.

With her cautious fingers she pulled off the white plaster to reveal an aperture, a hole. Then she took my hand.

The two of us stood there facing the camera. We moved of course, but not more than the plum trees did in the wind. Minutes passed. Whilst we stood there, we reflected the light, and what we reflected went through the black hole into the dark box.

It'll be of us, she said, and we waited expectantly.

7

[2]

Woman with a Dog on Her Lap

When it comes to my imagination, Angeline – as might be expected of her – is obstinately independent. Try as I do, I cannot imagine her as a young woman. And try as I do, I cannot really accept that she's now dead, that she's been dead for three years.

She keeps on watching me. I always amused her, the more so when I wasn't trying to, and now that she's dead she laughs out loud – even if silently! She knew she was going to play this trick, of course. It belonged to one of her secret plans, which she used to work out when she couldn't sleep at night, and when, the following morning, she had to tell a lie in order to communicate the enormity of the night she'd passed through. The lie was that she hadn't once closed her eyes.

When she took off her glasses, her eyes were no longer hard but full of wonder, and so it's difficult to explain why I could never imagine her young. Once she had a swollen knee and she asked me to rub some pomade on to it: her knees and thighs were as soft as a young bride's. When she undid her plaits, her white hair was abundant and fell down to her shoulder-blades. On the rare occasions when I kissed her – to wish her a Happy New Year, for example – she always pulled both of us into a corner, so that we should not be seen. Yet despite these things, I could not imagine her young.

9

I suppose the explanation was her mourning. When you put on black – and she wore black for thirty years – you put youth behind you for ever. I remember a man on a bicycle saying when the traffic had to stop to let a wedding cortège pass: the sign of the newlywed is a young woman at an open window with a duvet in her arms, and the sign of widowhood is an old woman alone chopping firewood with an axe.

Angeline was happy more often than she cared to admit. Coming back from the forest loaded with dead wood to chop, she was happy. In principle, she tried not to laugh in public: it was not appropriate to the black she wore. Covertly, she was happy when she made someone else laugh. And she had a gift of repartee which was inimitable. Her tactic was to cut, as with a knife, what she had just heard and then to make a bow with it. He's got billy-goat shit in his pockets, she said of Giscard d'Estaing on the screen. Every morning, except on Sundays, I used to hear the postman laughing in her kitchen for ten minutes. Sometimes with me she would let herself laugh. *Jésu, Marie, et Joseph, comment tu es bête!* she would say.

She was in mourning for her husband but more for her son, who had been killed in a road accident when he was in his early twenties. Her suffering then – and she clasped this suffering thirty years because it was all

10

that was left of her son which she could clasp – gave her a sense of solidarity with anybody else who was suffering. She visited the sick. She visited the bereaved. Her suffering sought the suffering of others so that they could stand side by side.

On several occasions she asked me how to send cash to the television to buy food to send to a country she had seen the night before where people were starving.

At the same time she had a deep feeling for luxury. She owned three goats, she needed to count her money, and she lived in a space of no more than fifty square metres, but she could imagine luxury. This was why her most loving insult was *feignant* – which means idle. Her dog and her goats were *feignant*. And she said I risked to be so. When Angeline was young, idleness in the village was the summit of luxury.

Her dog was called Mickey after the Mouse. Small, black, noisy and silly. A dog who never grew up. She swore at him. She locked him out. When he was sick he hid under the stove which she polished twice a week. But when he was bitten by another dog she nursed him on her lap as Calypso nursed Odysseus.

And Angeline waited until this morning to play the trick on me.

Certain villages appear to have come into being haphazardly – like dice thrown across a table. The reason for other villages is more obvious: they were built where two valleys meet, or where a river narrows. Yet others look as though they were the result of a sleight of hand, as if, from the beginning, from the very choice of their site, they had the pretension to show something off. As if the village was built from *flair*! Our village is of this last kind.

It looks happier than it is. The church has a fine steeple. The cemetery is like a balcony above it. The *Mairie* with its *tricolore* stands back from and above the road – almost with the stance of a château. The two cafés – including the Républicain Lyre – have steps leading up to them. And on the hillside behind, the farms are arranged like loges in a gigantic green theatre.

I was thinking about this as I approached the village this morning in the winter sunlight. A lot has changed recently, but from a distance in the winter sunlight, it might still be the village it was at the beginning of the century. And suddenly this morning I saw it like that. It was different from the ten thousand other times I'd seen it. It was full of mysterious promises.

I knew I would be married in its church, I knew that my children would go to its school, that my husband would take the mare each spring on March the 14th to be blessed by the *Curé*. It was at that moment I heard her silent laughter. It was she who had been looking at the village, not I, and she had made me see it through her eyes. And she was laughing because she had made me see it through her eyes when young.

[3]

Passenger to Omagh

There's a painting by Jack Yeats which shows a woman bare-back rider, a rider of the *haute école*, with her thoroughbred horse, and she's talking to a clown who sits hunched up on a box near the entrance to the Big Top. It's entitled: *That Grand Conversation Was Under the Rose*.

When Jack Yeats was very old, I spent an evening with him in Dublin. An unforgettable evening of stories and whiskey. I didn't ask him then because I didn't know I would need it, but thirty years later (he'd be 125 years old today) I fancy he'd agree if I borrowed his title for the duration of a bus ride.

Out of season between Dublin and Derry there are two buses a day. The road crosses the right shoulder of Ireland. In December, when we took the bus, there was a small rain and the stone walls and the cattle in the irregular fields were drenched. Snug in our seats, we were sucking peppermints and reading yesterday's newspapers from Paris. She got on at Castleblaney. Carrying a plastic carrier bag, she walked down the aisle and took one of the empty seats.

I noticed her on account of her face and its unusual expression. She reminded me, not of an animal, but of some picture of one. Perhaps of the lion who became the companion of Mark, the Evangelist. Sometimes this lion has an expression on his face which, at the same time, is smiling, wounded and a little mocking.

The bus moves off. She hears us talking in French and, after a while, she turns and asks:

Where are you from?

She is squat and short so she has to lean out over the aisle in order to see us round the back of her seat.

You weren't born here, she goes on, you're strangers.

Her eyes are unexpectedly light and they are blue.

So you're going to Derry, she continues, and I'm going to Omagh. Are you on holiday?

We're working in Derry with some actors.

I'm going to be in a play too! Why don't you come and sit beside me?

She moves so that the seat beside her is free. I sit beside her and she tells me her name is Kathleen and I ask her what play she's in.

A Christmas Carol. My first role, when I was very small, was the infant Jesus. Two years back it was the Lady Macbeth I played.

Very different, I say, very different. So you want to be an actress?

It was probably then that she calculated that I was a little stupid.

I'm going to be a hairdresser.

In Omagh?

No, I'm at school in Omagh. I've been home for the weekend. I'm sixteen. Were you taking me for being older?

A little.

It happens.

You have brothers and sisters?

We're five but we have different fathers. Now Mum lives with Bill. He's younger than she is and she's pregnant.

Is the baby due soon?

In April. I get on with Bill, he's easy. I'm pregnant as well.

I see.

Mine is for the month of May.

You'll both have your babies in the same hospital?

Yes, we will. We like the nurses there. And who knows, they may have got the dates wrong, we could overlap.

Mum and you?

Yes.

And the father, the father of yours?

He didn't want the baby. Get rid of it! he told me. I wouldn't hear of it. I want our baby and I'm keeping it! So he left. Now he's living with my oldest girlfriend.

Not very loyal, I say.

Ach! He's only seventeen, poor kid. And I have the baby, I'm happy. I want to have lots of children. Shall I be showing you the birthday card I bought for my sister?

She finds an envelope in the carrier bag and hands it to me.

She'll be furious I haven't bought her a present, my sister. I wanted to get her a book. Maybe the latest by Roddy Doyle. But I didn't have the money, so she'll just have to smile at my card, won't she? Go on, open it!

On the card is a picture of a white rose and underneath it the written words: To Deirdre with love from Kathleen.

She stays at home, my sister. She's ten years older than me and she doesn't go out at all. She's written a book.

I offer Kathleen a peppermint.

She looks with her bright eyes from under her lowered eyelids. Would it be bothering you if I smoked?

I point towards her belly.

She lays her hand on my arm to reassure me. I know, she says, I'm going to stop at the end of the week. The heroine of my sister's book is called Annie. She gets raped and becomes pregnant. The man, who is old enough to be her father, throws her

18

downstairs hoping she'll miscarry. She lies there and pretends to be dead and when he bends over her, she grasps him – you can guess where – and pulls and pulls until he's howling. At this moment one of his mates comes in through the front door and the two of them decide –

Is this what happened to Deirdre? I ask.

What in the name of God makes you say that? No, no. Her father, he wasn't my father as I told you, he interfered with her when she was little – but that's all, nothing more. The tragedy for Deirdre is she's deaf. She can't hear a thing. She's stone deaf.

She was born like that?

A car accident ... I was in California at the time.

California?

We're having a grand talk, aren't we? she says.

You remember where you were in California?

A place called Lodi, fifty miles north of Oakland. You'll be in Derry by one.

She holds up the birthday card of the rose for us both to look at again.

This afternoon I'll be washing my hair, now do you think I might allow it to grow longer?

You could.

No, she says, and tucks the card into the net pocket of the seat in front, long hair is too hot in the summer. What's your favourite colour for roses?

Rose, I think.

I want you to be at ease. I've taken you away from your friends and maybe they don't like it. You don't have to stay, Johnny.

She fingers the birthday card.

Well, at school I share a room with Sheila. She's pregnant too. So we have an arrangement, one day I do everything for her and the next she does everything for me. Today it's her turn to look after me. So I'll wash my hair and then I'll see what's on the telly and then I'll learn my lines. I'm playing the Spirit of Christmas Past.

At this moment she pats her tummy. Her hand is plump with bitten fingernails.

Next year I won't be playing, I think. I'll have my baby to look after. Would you like to hear my first lines?

Go on.

'Bear but a touch of my hand there' – she places her hand near my heart – 'and you shall be upheld in more than this. Now your lip is trembling . . . and what is that upon your cheek? . . . these are but shadows of the things that have been . . .'

The bus stops at the gate of a cottage on a lonely road and an old couple get off, helping each other with their shopping. Behind the gate their dog is trying to jump over it.

For ten minutes neither Kathleen nor I speak.

I'm deaf too, she says eventually.

Come on, I say.

Not like Deirdre, I'm only deaf in one ear and you're sitting on the good side. In fact, I have a hearing-aid and I don't use it.

Another car accident?

No. It was a Friday night one year ago and I was pissed out of my mind and I got knocked down by a lorry. It broke my arm too.

She rolls up the sleeve of her cardigan and shows me a red weal by her shoulder.

If it's a boy, I'll call him Kevin and if she's a girl, Sara.

They didn't tell you, when they did the scan, whether it's a boy or a girl?

I didn't want to know, she says. I prefer mysteries. Do you like the names Kevin and Sara?

The bus stops twice in Omagh and at the second stop Kathleen gets to her feet, takes the birthday card of the rose from the net pocket of the seat and walks down the aisle without a word.

I watch her climbing a steep path towards a building which could be a school. She looks weighed down.

Sheila! she'll tell her girlfriend, I met a stranger on the bus and I spun him the tallest stories ever!

Did he believe you?

And Kathleen will nod her smiling and wounded and slightly mocking head.

[4]

A Man Wearing
a Lacoste Sweater

He was the last to enter the room. He was lean, tallish and in his mid-forties. He wore glasses and you immediately noticed his eyes. They were unusual because their look was both penetrating and sensitive. A man, you said to yourself, who calculated in millimetres. As he shook our hands, his smile of welcome revealed the same sense of precision concerning feelings. He knew the exact difference between acknowledgement and gratitude and between gratitude and delight. He smiled at us with a smile of acknowledgement. The circumstances of our meeting prevented him from adding: Please make yourselves at home.

We sat down, around the table. The room had no window. The other two prisoners were younger than he, one from Reunion Island and the second from Marseille. We introduced ourselves and began reading out loud the story we'd chosen.

The aim of incarceration is to reduce all exchanges with the world to a minimum. And this has an effect on voices. Ours, as we read, were unlike prisoners' voices. Our voices were volatile – like swallows in flight seen through a window. Maybe our voices were more interesting than the story we were reading.

Noises in a prison echo like sounds do in the hold of a ship. There's nothing to absorb or clothe them. Like prisoners, noises there have no privacy. So most of the

25

time you shut off your hearing – unless you choose to listen. If you so choose, then you listen sharply. The three men listened to our voices.

Over by the door of the room, the screw, who was leaning against the wall, read a comic. He had no need of voices. On the ring, chained to his belt, was a key to every door.

It was a love story we were reading. A story of passion, crime, interrogations, dream, death, forgiveness. Set in a faraway metropolis.

The boy from Reunion Island sat hunched up, frowning. The Marseillais leant back and looked as if he was alone, driving a car to the metropolis. On the sweater of the man with glasses, I suddenly noticed the Lacoste green crocodile trademark. A man of discernment. As we read, he nodded, as if acknowledgement was perhaps turning into gratitude.

In prison the imagination is caught by a form of genius which is seldom discussed or honoured outside. Every prisoner's imagination allots to this genius its particular value and place, but all imaginations identify with it. This is the genius required for escape, the genius of those few who make it 'over the hill'.

From the drawing-boards on which the penitentiary buildings were designed, for the most part a century ago, to the newly installed video cameras, from the metal landings outside the cell doors to the electronic alarm systems, from the obsessive suspicion of most of the screws to the Clausewitzian training of the Prison Directors, everything had been conceived and is run to make escape unthinkable. Day and night are systematically punctuated by routine or sadistic reminders of this unthinkability. Yet there are those who persist in thinking about it all the while. Of those, there are a few who try to translate thought into action. And of those few, a handful who – miraculously – succeed.

When a prisoner succeeds and makes it 'over the hill', those who remain inside dream and talk about the exploit as they would talk about a masterpiece. And masterpiece it is. An achievement, which in its imagination, ingenuity, discipline, persistence, planning and concentration, can compare with the bronze doors of the Sacristy in Florence by Donatello or Thelonius Monk playing *Epistrophy*.

By the entrance to the prison main-block, before the cage and the metallurgical detector, there was an office with a dozen video screens, monitored by a Dickless Tracy. She could bring in camera after camera as she chose, and she watched all day. Men exercising, men sleeping, men working, men grabbing, men shitting, men smoking, men waiting, men telling stories. She glanced at them all. Next to her telephone there was

27

an alarm bell. Every few minutes she checked what they were doing; what she couldn't know was what was being said.

Like every story told in prison, ours also offered a means of momentary escape. Insofar as one listened, one flew over the hill . . .

In the story we were reading, there was not only plot, suspense, dialogue, there was also everything which was normal, which belonged to waking up in everyday life out there, and which did not exist here. In the room without a window the story was a reminder of mountains, of silence, of dancing, of choosing which street to walk down, of privacy and its special gift which is intimacy, of deciding for oneself what to eat and when, of opening a window without a thought, of taking a train or a bath, of doors which nobody could see through . . .

The next time we paused, the man with glasses, his hands in the air like birds in flight, said: Very neat. And beautifully imagined. Really neat.

We went on with the story and the story went on reminding the three men. Before we reached the end, the screw interrupted us and held up his wrist watch as if he thought we might not understand what prison time was. It was over.

Thank you for the story, said the boy from Reunion.

The man with the glasses came over to me. He wanted more than ever to be a host. He spoke in a soft voice, as if he were somewhere else, by a garden gate, for example: I hope to see you again sometime . . . perhaps in another prison?

I nodded.

The warder took the three men down the corridor. The man with glasses and the Lacoste sweater turned round and made a vague sign with his hand.

[5]

An Old Woman
with a Pram

Near Oxford Circus, London. In the nineties. Difficult to judge her age, probably around forty-five. Her belongings were in a shopping chariot, lifted from a supermarket. She wheeled it along the pavement, her face slightly inclined, as if it were a pram and she were looking at a baby. Her belongings in the chariot were in plastic bags. She wore a scarf round her head and a fur hat – what the Russians call a chapka. Much of its fur had fallen out. She also wore trousers, a padded jacket and an imitation-fur coat, the colour of dust. From a distance you might think she was clothed like an Eskimo. Except for her feet. She was wearing a pair of American-style sneakers. She found them in a dustbin on New Cavendish Street, which is near Hallam Street where my mother once lived when she was alive.

In the London underground stations a number of platform benches have recently been replaced by a new piece of public furniture. A kind of perch – which allows waiting passengers to take the weight off their feet and thus lean back a little. Its notable advantage is that no tramp can lie down on it to sleep. At night when the woman with the chapka lies down on a piece of cardboard which she places on the station asphalt, she doesn't take off her white shoes but just loosens the laces so they don't pinch her feet, which swell up at night like my mother's did.

31

Now it is midday and she is walking towards a pedestrian precinct behind Oxford Circus where hundreds of pigeons gather. As soon as the pigeons perceive the woman with the chapka they waddle on their feet, or fly over the paving stones towards her. From her chariot she takes a black plastic bag of stale bread, thrown out by a restaurant in Mortimer Street, and breaking up the bread with her hands, she flings fistfuls of breadcrumbs into the air.

Several pigeons perch on her arms, a few hang, fluttering, in the air above her head, but most wait on the ground to peck up the crumbs as they fall. From time to time, absent-mindedly, the woman puts a scrap of bread into her own mouth.

During my childhood we had a stone birdbath in the back garden of our house and during one hard hard winter my mother – who must have been about the age of this woman at that time – strode every morning through the deep snow between the silver birch trees to put out toast on the frozen water. Like Maeterlinck, my mother believed birds carried messages from the dead. The tramp woman, holding a bird in her hands, is shooing the others away by tossing her head and prodding with her elbows into the air. The bird held against her breast has lost some of its feathers and its round head, a little smaller than a ping-pong ball, is half bald. It has refused the bread she offered. Still holding the pigeon against her coat, she searches in another one of her plastic bags and finds a baby's bottle with a teat and a little milk in it. She expresses a few drops into the pigeon's beak, which she manages to hold open.

Each day, before coming to Oxford Circus, she prepares the bald pigeon's bottle and each day, after feeding the rest of the flock, she gives the bald one its milk.

A crowd of shoppers from Oxford Street now stop to watch the woman with the chapka.

They can't see through the walls, can they? the homeless woman says to the bald bird. If they want to stare at the garden, let 'em!

Mummy!

[6]

A Young Woman
with Hand to Her Chin

When she entered a room full of people she had an almost Byzantine arrogance, like the Empress Theodora of Ravenna. She knew very well that, for such as her, self-defence began with the exclusion of any possibility of taking a liberty. And she made this exclusion unmistakably clear by both her expression and poise.

I say 'such as her' because she was a musician, she was an *émigré*, and the way a long, heavy skirt hung from her hips when she danced was biblical – it reminded you of generations of women without end.

She had been brought up by her grandmother, a country woman from the Ukraine. From her she had learnt how to kill chickens, feed geese and look after her own excited parents – her father was a concert cellist, her mother a pianist.

Under the tutelage of the grandmother she had acquired the confidence of an elder by the time she was twelve. Her first lover appeared when she was thirteen.

She could tell stories for a month. She had her own and her grandmother's fund to draw from. Funny, true, untrue. The stories all revealed how the world is made up of people who, like birds during a harsh winter, need to be fed in some way or another. Some were crows. Some were finches. When she told them she hunched herself up like an old woman peeling potatoes to cook in the soup. Her laugh – and she only laughed when you did – was light and silvery.

Concentrated on Beethoven's one-from-last piano sonata, she flushed as she played it and sweated like a farm girl. I will never again be able to separate the pathos of that sonata from the smell, like drying grass, of her sweat.

Once I started a drawing of her, just after she had been practising. The piano was still open and she was sitting nearby. I screwed up my eyes and I waited. The impulse of a drawing comes from the hand rather than the eyes. Perhaps from the right arm, as with a marksman. Sometimes I think everything is a question of aim. Even playing Opus 110.

Her left eye sometimes wanders, to become a fraction displaced. At that moment this slight asymmetry was the most precious thing I could see. If I could only touch it, place it, with my stub of charcoal without giving it a name . . .

She of course knew I was drawing her. She was sending something out to meet my aim. If what she sent out didn't miss my aim but touched it, there was a chance of a good drawing.

I've never known what likeness consists of in a portrait. One can see whether it's there or not, but it remains a mystery. For instance, photos never have a 'likeness'. The question isn't even asked about a photo. Likeness has little to do with features or proportions. Maybe it's what a drawing receives, if two aims touch like the tips of two fingers.

Gradually the drawn head on the paper did draw closer to hers. Yet now I knew it would never be close enough, for, as can happen when drawing, I had come to love her, to love everything about her, and no drawing, however good, can be more than a trace.

Sitting there, she told me a joke about the villagers in some country who were so mean that, when they went to bed, they stopped the clocks in their houses because that way the clocks would last longer!

I began to sense that the evolution of the drawing of her corresponded with another evolution. Each mark or correction I made on the paper was like something bequeathed to her before she was born. The drawing was dredging time. And its traces were, like chromosomes, hereditary ones.

I elect you as my other father, she said at exactly that moment.

I drew the hand holding the chin.

Finally, there was a kind of portrait, most of it rubbed out, which looked to me to be finished, so I handed it to her.

At first she glanced at it like the Empress Theodora. Then, as she studied it, she became completely herself and only twenty-one years old.

Can I take it? she asked.

Yes, Anyishka.

Two days later she returned to Odessa with her portrait, and I kept this photocopy.

[7]

A Man in One-Piece Leathers
and a Crash Helmet
Stands Very Still

The British privateer team, Phase One Endurance, riding a Kawasaki TT1, won the 24-hour endurance race at Liège earlier this year. And their first pilot Simon Buckmaster is at the moment placed third, according to points, in the World Endurance Championship. Tonight he could move up to first place. His co-pilots are Steve Manley and Roger Bennett.

It's the fourth hour of the Bol d'Or. Manley is racing, and Bennett is waiting in the pit to relieve him. It will be the second time since the start that Bennett will be out there, aiming, climbing over, tearing. Phase One is in seventh place at the moment. It's hot and so he has undone his one-piece leathers and is stripped to the waist. Out of respect nobody talks to him – any more than one would talk to a man praying.

To risk everything you have to withdraw from every contact. And if the solitude out there is not going to unnerve you, you have to slip into it early. He sprays water on to his torso and sits. He rotates his head to ease the neck muscles and the hypothalamus which controls saliva and all the adrenalin – for which there's no pit to refuel in.

He holds himself apart. The track with its thirteen bends and two zigzags is inscribed in his mind and in his arms like a cord with which you tie and untie knots.

41

He shakes his legs as if shaking off dust. Twenty-six times each lap, whilst cornering, he'll slide his loins over the saddle, knee ready towards the asphalt. Nobody talks to him.

A pilot friend enters and wordlessly, carefully, bandages Bennett's palms with tape to stop blistering. When the friend has gone, he takes the tape off and rebandages his hands. (I think of Glenn Gould wearing woollen mittens and playing Bach on a piano.) He slips plugs into his ears. Pulls on his helmet. Helmeted, at this moment, it is as if you have already left.

The mechanics place their hydraulic-jack in position, arrange two wheels ready for changing and check the petrol dump-tank. In the pit lane Bennett, helmeted, squats down on his heels in a riding position, his body anticipating the contours of the machine to be mounted. The No. 5, which will be his when he drives himself. Please God.

On the paddock side of the pits, up against the wire netting to keep the public out, a young woman with a small child in her arms, says: Look at Daddy! The little girl looks and doesn't react.

Manley drives in. Says one sentence to Bennett. At that hand-over frontier between pilots only the utterly essential is communicated. Bennett is away.

Manley comes out of his helmet. The little girl says: Daddy! His face is red, his long hair damp with sweat. Around his eyes there is the temporary disfigurement of any endurance pilot after twenty-five laps: as though the skin has been pulled back from the cheekbones and the eyelids no longer protect the eyes. He comes over to the wire and, pulling off his gloves, gives them to his daughter to play with.

The white leather over his left shoulder has been roughed and grazed. A few months back, he broke his collar-bone in a fall. Tenderly he touches the wire by his wife's face and begins to talk.

Afterwards when they come in, they have to talk because they have to come back out of the helmet. He talks, and later he follows his wife to take an improvised shower.

Buckmaster is preparing to go out there for the third time. He is alone. Bennett has been overtaken by a Ducati but there are already rumours that the Ducatis won't hold the pace. Buckmaster puts on his helmet and stands very still, waiting, small, a shearwater looking out to sea from a cliff edge.

The whine of Bennett coming in. Twenty seconds later the whine of Buckmaster leaving. Nightfall.

In their marquee the mother of all the Phase One team is cooking supper with a sauce bolognese for pasta. The news comes over the loudspeakers of a double spill – involving the Suzuki No. 3, the favourite in first place, and their own No. 5.

What happened? Nobody is sure. A racing accident. Here is one described by Sophocles around the year 450 BC:

> At each turn of the lap, Orestes reined in his inner trace-horse and gave the outer its head, so skilfully that his hub just cleared the post by a hair's breadth every time; and so the poor fellow had safely rounded every lap but one without mishap to himself or his chariot. But at the last he misjudged the turn, slacked his left rein before the horse was safely round the bend, and so fouled the post. The hub was smashed across, and he was hurled over the rail . . .

Come out alive from a crash there – it's a bad place, one of the mechanics in the marquee says, you're doing 240 km an hour, alive you're lucky.

Graziano, the Suzuki pilot, is pushing his bike back to the pits. No. 5 has abandoned the race. Simon

44

Buckmaster has not moved from the rail against which he was thrown.

A little later the surgeons at the hospital were unable to repair his severed leg; they had to amputate it below the knee.

[8]

Two Dogs
Under a Rock

I've known Tonio longer than any of my other friends. Almost half a century. Last year after we'd been unloading hay, and, hot and thirsty, were drinking cider with coffee, he began a story.

I've seen Antonin the shepherd cry twice. He was married. He didn't see much of his wife, shepherds are like soldiers in this way. She died, and he wept when he told me about her death. The second time I saw Antonin weep – well, I'll tell you.

The two men were in the valley of El Requenco, just north of Madrid. They never met elsewhere. On a large-scale ordnance map of the area you can find a building marked on the southern slope of the valley and beneath the little square are printed the words 'Casa Tonio'. Tonio took three years building it. It's not really a house, more like a cabin. Perched at an altitude of 1,000 metres on a mountainside of broken boulders and ilex trees, perched like a leaning tomb or like a man sitting at a corner of a table. When Tonio gets out of his Fiat van lower down the slope and starts the slow climb up to his cabin he walks exactly like a St Jérôme. He has hermit legs, long, thin, with inexplicably rounded knees, such as all hermits had. Around the cabin there is a dry-stone wall 4 metres high, forming a kind of corral which was built long ago to protect an apiary. Every year in May a lorry loaded with hives came along the dust road and men carried the hives to place them in the corral. For two months the bees made honey there. Otherwise, it is a place only for sheep, goats and lizards.

In May the gilo's in flower, says Tonio. The gilo is an ugly shrub but its white blossoms are everywhere like snow. Like manna from heaven.

Since he has had his pension, Tonio draws a lot in El Requenco. He draws the smashed rocks, the ilex, the sparse turf, the dry beds of torrents. Large black drawings in which he fits everything together as if the coiled surface of the earth at El Requenco were the shell of an immense and ancient tortoise. High above in the sky vultures circle. As he draws, he can hear their faint cries. Cries which imitate as if to encourage the last moans of some animal victim.

In El Requenco, bovids need shepherds. Antonin is short and square. On his feet he wears sandals cut out of old lorry tyres. Tyres which have been driven through a lot of goat shit. Antonin never learnt to read and has his own way of speaking.

By 'the great waters', he refers to the torrential rain provoked by frequent thunderstorms. He wears a black hat with the same pride as Solomon wore a crown. After days alone in the valley with his herd, the 'Casa Tonio' is, for Antonin when he spots it, like a photograph in a frame: a solemn reminder of otherwise forgotten occasions.

Both men alone in the valley defend themselves fiercely against encroaching intimacy. To smoke a cigarette sitting on one of the terraces where the hives used to stand, to drink a glass of water while they recount what they've seen on the mountainside during the last week, nothing more. And often when they sit, looking down the valley, they swear.

One day Antonin came by when Tonio was preparing a meal: potatoes with bacon. Tonio invited the shepherd to join him. The idea came to him without any reflection. He pronounced the invitation as if recounting a simple fact, like: last night I saw the badger. Antonin indicated his acceptance by taking off his hat and lowering his head. Tonio made a sign to suggest that the two dogs should stay outside.

When, however, the shepherd crossed the threshold into the single, unique room of the *casa*, something unforeseen by either of the two men occurred. One knew his way about blindfolded and the other did not. Tonio laid plates on the table, placed knives, forks and glasses beside them, fetched a flask of black wine, brought out the bread. Antonin leant back in his chair, speaking a sentence or two from time to time, talking of torrents, corrals, of names which were unfamiliar to

Tonio, but mostly he sat there silent, smiling, like a man having his hair cut in a café on a Sunday morning.

Tonio cut up tomatoes and trickled olive oil over them. The dogs outside found a place in the shade beneath a rock. When both men were at last seated, Antonin poured wine into their glasses. Otherwise, it was Tonio who served his guest.

They ate with gusto. Sometimes they'd lean back to talk. When they finished eating they went on drinking the black wine. Through the window, the valley in the afternoon heat looked as cruel as ever. Finally, Antonin put on his hat and, after fumbling for ten minutes in his pocket, he drew out a 1,000-peseta note which he slipped discreetly on to the table.

You can't do that! Tonio remonstrated. You can't! It was my pleasure.

No man before in my life has ever served me at table, declared Antonin. It was like a great restaurant.

Pick it up! shouted Tonio. You are spitting on my pleasure.

Shit . . . began Antonin.

The other, with a shaking hand, held out the note across the table. Antonin hid the money in his pocket, took off his hat, and then he stood there, his two arms a little apart from his square body. Between the fingers of his left hand he held an unlit cigarette, with his right

50

he held a hat. He stood there motionless in the cabin and down his cheeks rolled tears.

Seeing Antonin, Tonio began to weep himself. Neither hid anything. The dogs watched and waited: their master with his back to the door and the other man on his feet as if turned to salt. For many minutes neither man moved. Then they slowly raised their arms and embraced.

[9]

A House Designed
by Le Corbusier

André is waiting to leave his house in the Paris suburb of Boulogne-Billancourt. He has always carried this house around in his head as an image of home; and for the last twenty-five years he has actually lived in it. The house, however, belongs to somebody else, a question of American lawyers.

Another *etán*! André declares. Perhaps the last, my one hundredth and twenty-fourth! *Etán* means 'transfer' in Russian. It was the word prisoners used in the Gulag when they were moved from one camp to another. Transfers were what the zeks dreaded most, yet they were frequent. The unknown seemed more threatening than the known, even when the latter was intolerable. The body, already exhausted, often found it fatally hard to adapt to different conditions. And with each transfer the little sticks of one's identity were scattered or broken and had to be reassembled or mended.

At first André resisted the notice to quit the house in Boulogne-Billancourt and barricaded himself in. Near the heavy metal gate, which gives on to the street, he kept a short-handled Russian spade. With an instrument like this, he said, I've seen quite a few beheaded.

For years he resisted. Then he changed his mind. Today he reckons that, if they find him there when they come, they will destroy everything they can lay their hands on out of spite. None of it is worth selling.

53

You could get nothing for it, he says, but to me these bits and pieces are eloquent. He winks with one of his astute, almond-shaped eyes.

A removal needs to be planned like an escape, he insists, no detail, however small, is unimportant. Every day he packs papers, bits of cloth, books, drawings, letters, newspaper cuttings, spare parts of God knows what, a plastic bottle for olive oil in the form of a Greek vase which once amused his mother – into cardboard boxes which he numbers. Like this he hopes to escape with everything before the transfer.

Previously he escaped eight times. And this was a fabulous record in Kolyma. From Boulogne-Billancourt it will be the ninth time. Once on the other side of the wire, he says, it's not tourism you think about! He'll be moving into a single room, measuring 5 metres by 3, on a fifth floor.

The house he has to leave was designed by Le Corbusier in 1923 for Berthe, André's mother, and his stepfather, a sculptor. With its studio wall of murky glass and the crumbling concrete of its flat roof, it looks today more like an abandoned garage from which the petrol pumps were long since taken away! Nevertheless, it's a question of American lawyers.

There is a double portrait of André's mother and stepfather painted by Modigliani in 1917: Berthe, who came from Moscow, is on the right and Jacques Lipchitz on the left. Sometimes I think I can see in the placing of Berthe's almond eyes a certain resemblance to André.

A stranger, judging by appearances, could mistake André for a Renault salesman who retired last year. At seventy-eight he is remarkably spry, wiry and young for his age.

Inside the house there is a spiral staircase leading to the living quarters. The first room which gives off it is a bedroom, made to measure for André when he was a boy. Over the bed now hangs a painting which depicts a *Steppenwolf* in the snow. My portrait, jokes André, nodding towards the wolf.

So it's my last transfer and it makes me think of my first. Before I knew what transfers meant? I was fourteen. I caught the train from the Gare du Nord, accompanied by Lounatcharski, the People's Minister of Education! Mother had arranged this. When the train was leaving Berlin, the Minister's mistress suddenly remembered she hadn't bought all the underwear she meant to buy – ah! the secret world! – so she stood up, I was there in the same compartment, and she pulled down the chain for an emergency stop. The train jerked to a halt. And the men played cards till she came back with her shopping . . . Thirty-one years later when I had been rehabilitated and Lounatcharski was dead, I saw her on my return to Moscow, an old woman in a black dress.

After Berlin, Warsaw, Brest Litovsk, and Minsk, I arrived in Moscow on the morning of the tenth anniversary. November the 7th, 1927.

I went straight to the Red Square to watch the military march past, and to see my father for the first time in my life. He was on the podium in his general's uniform taking the salute! I stared up at him but the temperature was -28 and I could think of nothing except how cold I was. I was dressed as if I was going to the Lycée in Paris – my light suit with plus fours, a fashionable white raincoat with dark amber buttons and a pair of shoes with thick, spongy rubber soles. I was conspicuous and I was frozen to death.

Some officers behind the podium noticed me and took pity. At that time I didn't much speak Russian. One of them approached my father and, whispering, asked him what should be done. Wrap him up in a tarpaulin and deliver him to my house! he ordered. And this is what happened. They rolled me into an army-issue tarpaulin, dumped me in a side-car and pushed me through the front door. My stepmother thought I was a new carpet! Eventually she thought she heard the carpet murmuring! Soon afterwards I moved out of their house. For two years I was a vagabond and by the winter of '30 I was already an enemy of the people. My father the General was executed in '37.

Around the house in Boulogne-Billancourt there are many blocks of uncarved stone and marble. Lipchitz left for America in 1940 and never returned. By the back door there's usually a blue enamel plate brimming over with cat biscuits. For the birds, explains André, they nibble them . . . you see that cherry tree? It grew by itself one year after Mother died. When she was alive she had a habit of spitting out cherry stones from the living-room window. She particularly liked the Morello cherry.

In 1946 when the war was over, Berthe insisted upon leaving New York and coming back to the house in Paris: Somewhere my son's alive, I feel it, she said, and when he's released he'll go to the house in Boulogne-Billancourt to find me, and if I'm not there when he arrives, we'll never meet again on this earth.

She came back alone, and she had to wait fourteen years for André to return and to sleep again in the room made to his measure when he was a boy. By that time he was forty-five, he had spent twenty-seven years in the Gulag and he had been transferred one hundred and twenty-four times.

The son looked after the mother till she died.

In Paris he earned his living selling life-insurance policies.

One of the first things he did on his return was to put a tennis ball into a net bag and hang it on a tree, 20 centimetres from the ground. It was for his mother's cats to play with. It is still hanging there.

Packing one of the cardboard boxes, he finds a water-colour, pauses and holds it out at arm's length. It's better than I thought when I did it, he says, do you want it? The water-colour shows an alpine chalet in summertime. Around the chalet stand stooks of hay. It was clearly done, like a child's painting, from imagination, not on the spot. Yes, I'd like it.

I'll sign it, he says, and on the reverse side of the paper, in large loose script, he writes: 'My dear John – in recollection of my marvellous August holidays, 1905, spent in your mountain chalet – André.'

As he writes he bites his lip to stop himself laughing out loud and spoiling the joke. In 1905 none of us had been born and none of us had been transferred even once.

[10]

A Woman
on a Bicycle

The bulbs in their bowl on the kitchen windowsill are putting out shoots. Sometimes the shoots of potatoes, motivated as gimlets, thrust their way through cardboard and even wood in their search for light when spring comes. If the bulbs on the windowsill are the same as she sent last year, they will flower as miniature narcissi. Each flower no larger than a thumbnail. With a sweetly pungent perfume – almost like that of a dying animal. Flowers of the north. Reindeer flowers.

In the kitchen cupboard there's a home-made honey cake which she also sent. Heaven knows what the recipe is. Like a treacle tart, but instead of treacle, a mixture of honey and grated nuts. Perhaps hazel nuts? Anyway, the last nuts one might find when travelling north to Lapland.

On the table are some African toffees. I may be wrong. It may be that only the wicker casket the toffees are in came from Africa. (There was a label inside which said Uganda.) The toffees themselves, each one wrapped evidently by hand, soft and black, were more likely made in her kitchen in Göteborg.

It is also thanks to her that, a few years ago, I discovered Torgny Lindgren. In one of the parcels she sent she included *Mehrab's Beauty* – the best story ever written about a cow. After this I read everything by Lindgren. In the letter inside the parcel she wrote:

I am sitting on the ferry for Denmark. We are leaving Göteborg through the long harbour passage – oil depots – everything is changed. The inner harbour is in a way dead, no shipbuilding any more, only those big 'hotel-ferries' for Denmark and Germany, all private. I hate to travel by these 'sea-hotels' but it is the only possibility – and I always go as a 'free passenger'. I hurry on board at the very last minute with my bike and no ticket! It's a gloomy sky, about -4C. In the north, where I was born, I heard on the radio it's -30C.

This was the woman who, one April afternoon, was riding a bicycle along a narrow country road near the Lac du Bourget, not far from Aix-les-Bains. The lake is famous because of the poem of Lamartine:

Ainsi, toujours poussés vers de nouveaux rivages,
Dans la nuit éternelle emportés sans retour,
Ne pourrons-nous jamais sur l'océan des âges
  Jeter l'ancre un seul jour?

The bicycle was one of those upright models such as elderly professors ride in university towns. And she indeed is a teacher: she teaches Swedish literature to refugee students – particularly Iranians and Ugandans.

The bicycle, however, had been transformed. Not by changing its handlebars, saddle or pedals: all its parts were the same, even the brake fittings, each one like a snaffle bit from a horse's bridle. The transformation was the result of what the bike carried. The rear mudguard was draped, like a camel's loins, with saddle bags. A tent, an umbrella and a water bottle were strapped on to the back carrier. In the front basket, under the battery lamp, were maps, lotions, a bag of dried figs, candles, a hammer and a new book by Lindgren.

This woman with curly grey hair was pedalling slowly along a narrow country road near the Lac du Bourget, slowly but everlastingly. A black Peugeot 605 approached, driving in the same direction as the woman on the bicycle. The Peugeot driver was telephoning one of his partners. He miscalculated the narrowness of the lane and the rear of the car brushed against the cyclist's right saddle bag. This precipitated both bicycle and rider into the ditch.

The car didn't stop. For an accident, a collision, to be registered, a certain weight has to be involved. Nobody thinks of stopping when a butterfly hits the windscreen. And the shock felt in the Peugeot was no greater than that.

The woman swore, picked herself up and examined the damage. First to her bicycle, then to herself. The front wheel was buckled and the left pedal was hurt. As for herself, she had a cut on her knee. The skin of her legs was smooth, almost like marble. Perhaps a lifetime's wading in sea water might have this effect on the skin. The flowing blood was dark. She tied a rag around her knee and sat on the edge of the road to wait for the next motorist. It was a baker's van. The driver stopped and took her to Yenne. There her bicycle could be repaired.

The next morning when, with a new front wheel and a bandaged knee, she took to the road, coming north, it began to rain.

She was wearing a waterproof army cape when she arrived in the village. I was first struck by her blue eyes. They say blue eyes age less than dark ones. And the eyes in her weathered face were those of a young girl. Later I learnt that she had been married and had two grown-up children. We hung up her shirt to dry over the kitchen stove and we ate soup and cheese. Afterwards she unbandaged her knee and I saw the little wound.

It'll be healed in three days, she said.

She went outside, rummaged in the front basket of her bicycle, and held out a jam jar.

Some quince jelly, she announced, it's for you. I'll be going, but first, if I may, I'll take a little walk.

64

She leant her bicycle against the outdoor stairs. When she came back half an hour later, she had a package of primroses with their roots which she carefully arranged in her front basket.

It's a bit late now to go so far, I said.

Sometimes I ride by night.

You're not frightened?

I have my bicycle!

When she started off down the road, she waved but did not look back. She was pedalling slowly and everlastingly. A vagrant with no need to beg but a need to give.

$$\left[11 \right]$$

A Man Begging
in the Métro

It's all a question of time, he says.

I watch him. He is eighty-six and he looks much younger, as if he had a special contract with time passing. His eyes are an intense pale blue, and from time to time they twitch, as a dog's muzzle twitches when investigating a scent. It's hard to watch his eyes without feeling you're being indelicate. They're totally exposed – not through innocence, but through an addiction to observation. If eyes are windows on to the soul, his have neither panes nor curtains, and he stands in the window frame and you can't see past his gaze.

Monet and Renoir, he says, painted the view from this window here. They were friends of Victor Chocquet who lived in the flat below.

Chocquet, the man Cézanne painted a portrait of, with a gentle thin face and a beard? I say.

Yes, he says, Cézanne painted several portraits of Chocquet. Here's a reproduction of the Monet of the Palais Royal. You see how the spire there nicks into the dome, closer than a tangent? Now look out of the window. It's the same. He painted from exactly this spot . . . Photography doesn't interest me any more.

If he was an animal, I think he'd be a hare; all the time he's on the point of bounding away. Not in flight. Not in mockery. But casually, for the hell of it. Instead

67

of ears which bring him the news about everything, he has eyes. Amused eyes.

The only thing about photography that interests me, he says, is the aim, the taking aim.

Like a marksman?

Do you know the Zen Buddhist treatise on archery? Georges Braque gave it to me in '43.

I'm afraid not.

It's a state of being, a question of openness, of forgetting yourself.

You don't aim blind?

No, there's the geometry. Change your position by a millimetre and the geometry changes.

What you call geometry is aesthetics?

Not at all. It's like what mathematicians and physicists call elegance, when they're discussing a theory. If an approach is elegant it may be getting near to what's true.

And the geometry?

The geometry comes in because of the Golden Section. But calculation is useless. Like Cézanne said: 'When I start thinking, everything's lost.' What counts in a photo is its plenitude and its simplicity.

I notice the small camera on the table beside him, within easy reach.

I gave up photography twenty years ago, he says,

to go back to painting and above all to drawing. Yet people keep on asking me about photography. A while back I was offered an award for my 'creative career as a photographer'. I told them I didn't believe in such a career. Photography is pressing a trigger, bringing your finger down at the right moment.

He imitates the gesture comically in front of his nose. And, as I laugh, I remember the Zen Buddhist tradition of teaching by jokes, of refusing anything ponderous.

Nothing is lost, he says, all that you have ever seen is always with you.

Did you ever want to be a pilot?

Now it's his turn to laugh because I've guessed right.

I was doing my military service in the Air Force, stationed at Le Bourget. Not far away, towards Paris, was the family factory. The well-known Cartier-Bresson reels of cotton! So they knew I was the kid son of a bourgeois. I was put to sweeping out the hangars with a broom. Then I had to fill out a form. Did I want to be an officer? No. Academic achievements? None, I wrote, because I hadn't passed my *baccalauréat*. What were my first impressions of military service? I replied by quoting two lines from Jean Cocteau:

don't go to so much trouble

      the sky belongs to us all . . .

This, I thought, expressed how I wanted to be a pilot.

I was called before the commanding officer who asked me what the hell I meant. I said I was quoting the poet Jean Cocteau. Cocteau what? he shouted. He went on to warn me that, if I wasn't pretty careful, I'd be drafted to Africa in a disciplinary battalion. As it was, I was put into a punishment squad in Le Bourget.

He has picked up the camera and is looking at me – or, rather, around me, as if I had an aura, as he speaks.

When I was demobilised, I went to the Ivory Coast and earned my living there hunting game. I used to shoot at night with a lamp on my head like a coal miner. There were two of us, and my companion was an African. Then I fell ill with blackwater fever. I'd have certainly died but I was saved by my brother hunter who was skilled, like a medicine man, in the use of herbs. He had already poisoned a white woman because she was too arrogant. Me, he saved. He nursed me back to life . . .

As he tells me this story, it reminds me of other stories I've heard and read about lost travellers being brought back to life by nomads and hunters. When they're brought back, they're not the same. Their sign has been changed by an initiation. The following year,

Cartier-Bresson bought his first Leica. Within a decade he was famous.

The geometry, he is now saying, comes from what's there, it's given to one, if one is in a position to see it.

He puts down the camera he was pointing at me without using it.

I want to ask you something, I say, please be patient.

Me? I can't help it. I'm impatient.

The instant of taking a picture, I persist, 'the decisive moment' as you've called it, can't be calculated or predicted or thought about. OK. But it can easily be lost, can't it?

Of course, for ever. He smiles.

So what indicates the decisive split-second?

I prefer to talk about drawing. Drawing is a form of meditation. In a drawing you add line to line, bit to bit, but you're never quite sure what the whole is going to be. A drawing is an always unfinished journey towards a whole . . .

All right, I reply, but taking a photograph is the opposite. You feel the moment of a whole when it comes, without even knowing what all the parts are! The question I want to ask is: Does this 'feeling' come from a hyper-alertness of all your senses, a kind of sixth sense –

The third eye! He puts in.

– or is it a message from what is in front of you?

He chuckles – like hares do in folk tales – and leaps away to look for something. He comes back holding a photocopy.

Here's my answer – by Einstein.

The quotation has been copied out in his own handwriting. I read the words. They are taken from a letter of Einstein's addressed to the wife of the physicist Max Born in October '44. 'I have such a feeling of solidarity with everything alive that it doesn't seem to me important to know where the individual ends or begins . . .'

That's an answer! I say. Yet I'm thinking about something different. I'm thinking about his handwriting. It's large, easy to read, open, rounded, continuous, and surprising.

When you look through the view-finder, he says, whatever you see, you see naked.

His handwriting is surprising because it's maternal, it couldn't be more maternal. Somewhere this virile man who was a hunter, who was co-founder of the most prestigious photo-agency in the world, who escaped three times from a prisoner-of-war camp in Germany, who is a maverick anarchist and Buddhist, somewhere this man's heart is that of a mother.

Check it with his photos, I tell myself. Check it against the men in bowler hats, the abattoir workers, the lovers, the drunks, the refugees, the tarts, the judges, the picnickers, the animals and, on every continent, the kids, above all the kids.

Only a mother can be that unsentimental and love without illusion, I conclude. Maybe his instinct for the decisive moment is like a mother's instinct for her offspring, visceral and immediate. And who really knows whether this is instinct or message?

Of course the heart, maternal or otherwise, doesn't explain everything. There's also the discipline, the persistent training of the eye. He shows me a painting by Louis, his favourite uncle, a professional artist who was killed in Flanders during the First World War, aged twenty-five. We examine other drawings by his father and grandfather. Topographical landscapes of places they found themselves in. A family tradition, passed from generation to generation, of minutely observing branches and patiently drawing leaves. Like embroidery, but with a male, lead pencil.

When he was nineteen, Henri went to study with André Lhote, the Cubist master. And there he learnt about angles, walls and the way things tilt.

Some of the drawings, I say to him, some of your still lifes and Paris street-scenes make me think of Alberto Giacometti. It's not an influence so much as the two of you sharing something. You both share, in your

73

drawings, a way of squeezing between a table and a chair, or between a wall and a car. It's not you physically, of course. It's your vision that slips through to the other side, to the back –

Alberto! he interrupts. Despite all the hell of this life, a man like him makes you realise it's worth being alive. Yes, we slip through . . .

He has picked up his camera and is looking at what is around me again. This time he clicks.

Slipping through, he says. Take coincidences, there's no end to them. Maybe it's thanks to them we glimpse an underlying order . . . The world has become intolerable today, worse than the nineteenth century. The nineteenth century ended in about 1955, I think. Before, there was hope . . .

He has bounded away again to the edge of the field.

We look together at a photo he has just taken of the Abbé Pierre. It's an image which shows the compassion, the fury and the godliness of that remarkable man who fights for the homeless and is the most loved public figure in France. Photographer and priest must be about the same age. A picture of one tireless old man taken by another. And if the Abbé's mother could see Pierre today, she'd see him, I think, as he is at this instant in this photo.

Finally I say I must leave.

People ask me about my new projects, he says, smiling. What shall I say to them? To make love tonight. To do another drawing this afternoon. To be surprised!

I take the lift down from the apartment on the fifth floor and I think he may do another drawing.

In the Métro I find a seat in a coach which is more than half full. At the end of the coach, a man in his early forties makes a short speech about his handicapped wife whom he is leading by the hand and who follows him with her eyes shut. They've been turned out of their lodgings, he says, and they risk to be separated if they apply to any institution.

You don't know, the man tells the coach, what it's like loving a handicapped woman – I love her most of the time, I love her at least as much as you love your wives and husbands.

Some passengers give him money. To each one the man says: *Merci pour votre sensibilité.*

At a certain moment during this scene I suddenly glanced towards the door, expecting him to be there with his Leica. This gesture of mine was instantaneous and without reflection.

Photography, he once wrote in his maternal handwriting, is a spontaneous impulse which comes from *perpetually* looking, and which seizes the instant and its eternity.

75

[12]

Sheets of Paper
Laid on the Grass

Many months afterwards, Marisa Camino sent me a print of the photo taken under the plum tree. Our traces remain, yet they are far less substantial than those of the tree and they are two-faced: it would be hard for a third person to decide whether we were leaving or returning, were in the process of appearing or disappearing, whether we were alive or were ghosts. With the photo was a letter and a telephone number.

And so the next summer I found myself sitting on the grass outside a small house in Galicia, about twenty kilometres from the sea. Marisa's lightweight racing bicycle was leaning against the outside wall of the house beside the front door. The kitchen was just large enough for four of us to sit round a table and eat for supper the clams she'd cooked.

Next to the kitchen was a narrow hallway where she brought in the bicycle at night and stacked several of her larger paintings. All the ceilings of the house were covered with rolls of milkily transparent plastic which she had stapled up to prevent dust, made by woodworms, continually falling from the devoured floorboards and beams – the house was probably a century old – on to papers or food or hair.

Sitting on the grass we could hear a neighbour's chickens and some pigeons in a pigeon loft. There were no clouds, the August sun in the west was going down very slowly and the light was diffused and vast – as though reflected by the entire Atlantic. She was taking drawings from a portfolio she had brought downstairs. The house had four rooms if you counted the bathroom. The drawings were wrapped in tissue paper like folded clothes. Methodically, one by one, she took them out of their wrapping and laid them on the grass. I pay 12,000 pesetas a month for the house, she had said.

There exist drawings which are investigative studies and others which are sketches for projected master-pieces. There are very many kinds of drawings. The ones now laid on the grass were written like letters.

The most notable collection of drawings of this kind – drawings written like letters – is to be found in the Kunstmuseum in Bern and they were made by Paul Klee between the years 1927 and 1940. (The years of my childhood; it was in 1940, the year of his death, that I first saw a painting by Klee reproduced.) They talk, these pencil drawings by Klee, of, amongst other things, the rise of fascism, his loves, his health and his foretold death. They are like letters because you have the feeling that they have been drawn without once looking up, and that the trusted one to whom they are addressed resides in the paper itself.

Behind the kitchen there is a kind of dark annexe – maybe, originally, chickens were shut in there at night

– and this is where Marisa makes her paper. She makes it from straw which she soaks in water, lets ferment and then presses out. The paper is camel-coloured (she says 'rabbit-coloured'), full of fibres like bread. Besides sometimes using this paper for drawing, she makes envelopes with it. The photo she sent to me came in one of these envelopes.

Most of Klee's drawings concerned ideas – ideas which could only be defined with pencil lines for they came from the right hemisphere of the brain. Although he drew plants, birds, animals, he was not directly intimate with nature. It was through the workings of the human brain that he discovered nature. Ideas flowed through the lead of his pencil on to the paper and he pursued them upstream back into the circuits, the galleries of the brain, and it was in those networks that he got close, very close, to the forms and rhythms of nature. But his drawings were about thinking. The ones on the grass are about feeling.

When she draws she is perhaps almost mindless. She too makes her way upstream, but not towards a brain, rather towards the pre-Cambrian, the era of the first molluscs (like the clams we'll eat for supper). She learns about her nature from medusas, cuttle fish, octopus, limpets, gastropods, who have been around for nine-tenths of the period during which there has been life on our planet. She also learns from sandhoppers and sea-horses.

When I first met her, I thought of the Mustelidae and *belettes*. I was wrong. Her drawings go further back.

My yellow van, she told me earlier, caught fire when I skidded into a wall on a wet road. Nobody stopped. I had to rescue my things myself. I got my drawings out. Only a few pages were burnt at the edges. Now I have a Volkswagen. And she grinned.

Upstairs there is a room she uses as an atelier for her work as a restorer. At the moment she is repairing a broken wooden scroll from a golden altar and a seventeenth-century painted statue of a Madonna. Her work is meticulous and – like that of all good restorers – almost invisible, as though no hand of hers had touched the thing restored.

There is a drawing, not by her, but by Klee, called *Cowardly Dog*. It shows a dog cringing before a stork-like bird. The animal's cowardice is expressed through the very scribbles which confuse the contours of its body. For Klee every sensation passed through his drawing hand. In the making of her drawings there is apparently no hand.

Often they are in colour and have been made with a brush. Sometimes scraps of other things – leaves, feathers, cloth, different kinds of paper – have been glued on to the drawing. But, never do you feel the creator's hand. Only the appetite of the plant or creature represented. A shrimp eats. A spore germinates. A special worm extracts calcium carbonate from sea water. Lichen both shelters and devours its algae. Such are the facts I look up afterwards.

At the moment I sit on the grass peering at the sheets of paper. The sun is going down and the sudden change of temperature over the land but not over the ocean has provoked a breeze. A wisp of grass is blown on to one drawing. Tiny fruit flies alight on another. A scrap of leaf, transparent like parchment, drifts from a nearby field of maize on to another sheet. If I did not see these things being wafted on to the paper I would mistake them for painted marks. I'm no longer at all sure where to draw the line between art and nature, Becoming and Origin. This is the mystery that keeps me peering, even after the light has dimmed and the chickens have gone quiet.

Marisa Camino comes out of the house to tell me supper is ready.

As soon as I finish the church in La Coruña, she says, I'm going to Stromboli. There's nothing on the island of Stromboli – did you see the film? – not even a hotel, nothing except the volcano, and I want to look into it many times.

$$\left[\,13\,\right]$$

Psalm 139:

'. . . you know me when I sit
and when I rise . . .'

Psalm 139

I will praise thee

for I am fearfully
and wonderfully made :
marvelous are thy works
and that my soul knoweth right well
My substance was not hid from thee
when I was made in secret
                and curiously wrought
                in the lowest parts
                of the earth

Thine eyes did see my substance
yet being imperfect
and in thy book
all my members were written
which in continuance were fashioned
when as yet was none of them

[14]

Street Theatre

I hadn't visited Barcelona for many years. It was the end of March and in vacant lots on the outskirts of the city the first red poppies were in flower. Summer was approaching. The sun was high enough in the sky to penetrate the alleys, no wider than a mule is long, running between the five-storey buildings which make up the district around the basilica of Santa Maria del Mar, in the centre of the old city, a little back from the waterfront.

Some of the buildings here were once palaces; all of them have thick walls and staircases of worn stone. Around them on the ground, like hair on the floor of a barber's shop, is strewn the debris of daily life. The old gateways are shut with heavy metal doors signed repeatedly by tag artists.

Old women in slippers come down to the streets to chat and buy three or four onions. The middle-aged ones argue more loudly and in the daytime often wear jogging suits. The young ones in mini-skirts flick their wrists, wriggle their fingers and claim their inalienable right to dismiss and disdain. In the afternoon there are few men about, except for the occasional one in a bar or an elderly husband walking arm in arm with his wife to a bench in the sun. The proper men arrive later. A pigeon sleeps on a windowsill, beak towards tail, head on breast.

In each street, from the upper windows under the blue sky, hangs washing. Lean out over the iron railing of the minuscule balcony and unpeg whatever is dry. If the neighbour on the opposite side of your street has washed a shirt, the shirt's arm, outstretched, could easily touch your pillowcase. I wander along the Carrer de Jaume Giralt, recalling many things, and particularly, her voice telling of Barcelona.

When the summer comes, on the days when the fire falls from the sky – El Cae Fuego – the lightest sheet here is unbearably hot as you lie on a bed. In the *canicule* heat everything becomes monolithic, stuck together – the walls, the metal, the air in the rooms, the iron railings, the table with washing on it, the pigeons, even the water in the pipes. The only way to forget the heat – for those who can – is to make love! The next best thing is to shift the air a little with a fan: the air will cool your ears.

During El Cae Fuego the streets are full of dreams of being on a small island somewhere else. You think of those you love who are lucky enough to be far away from this stifling port: Eduardo studying electronics, José who is in the mountains, Isabel who works in Paris. Wherever they are, they can breathe without thinking about it. Then you find yourself glancing at the clock as if it were a thermometer!

After midnight the fever always goes down a few degrees.

I have arrived at the Carrer Ferran and I turn left towards Las Ramblas. The first small green leaves have unfolded on the platan trees which line the great open walk leading from the Plaza Catalunya to the pillar of Columbus which looks out to sea.

Far away, in the middle of the esplanade, I spot something unusual. A man standing on a stepladder? In any case something or somebody a head or two taller than all those walking fast or strolling away from the sea or towards it.

When I get nearer I discover that the unusual tall thing is a scarecrow planted on an upturned box. The scarecrow – *el espantapájaros* – is facing the other way, so what I see is a blanket hanging, like a poncho, from a horizontal stick which represents the shoulders, a head of long straw hair and a hat. Perched on the hat stands a pigeon. The pigeon puzzles me for it is so still. Birds when they are not in the air, I say to myself, have a capacity for not moving which makes them more like reptiles than animals.

Strangely I don't ask myself what a scarecrow may be doing in Las Ramblas. On another day here you might come across Jacob Dreaming – why not? – or the hermit St Jérôme praying. Probably the scarecrow, I tell myself, is part of a publicity stunt for some American fast-food joint.

I am close enough now to see that the pigeon is not alive. It is a stuffed bird perching on the scarecrow's hat. I notice too that, beneath the blanket hanging like a poncho, the legs are a pair of blue jeans and the feet a pair of white sneakers. The fact that they are totally still now makes me wonder whether they are alive.

I walk round to the front and look up at the face. I see a man wearing glasses and a straw wig. Perhaps a student in his last year? His eyes stare fixedly ahead. Not an eyelash, not a nerve quivers. His arms are crossed against his chest like those of a corpse in a coffin.

When did I last look into a coffin? Eleven months ago. Already eleven months . . .

The man is not pallid, he is tanned, and the lines on his face are more visible than morticians usually allow on the faces of the dead. His eyes are open and he is staring down the whole length of Las Ramblas towards the sea.

Often during a vigil by an open coffin you have the impression that the mouth of the deceased moves. The impression raises no hope, it is merely a reminder that the departed has not yet gone very far. With her it was her eyelids.

I stand and watch *el espantapájaros* and the minutes

pass. Five, ten . . . Not a muscle moves. A breath of wind from the sea stirs some of the straws of long hair by his left shoulder. Does he know I've been watching him for so long? I ask myself. She didn't know, thank God. She was still very near but she didn't know.

A small boy followed by his mother runs down the esplanade towards us. On the pavement in front of the upturned box the scarecrow has placed a red plastic bowl with some coins in it. The boy stops and drops a 100-peseta piece into the bowl. *El espantapájaros* slowly lifts his left hand in a sign of acknowledgement, lowers his head a few degrees and smiles at the boy. The solemnity of the gesture reminds me of certain painted Resurrections in which the four soldiers are asleep by the tomb, and Christ, lifting his left hand in blessing, rises up.

Now he is acting dead again. The most difficult minutes for sustaining his stillness must, I think, be the minutes – like these – just after he has moved.

I would love to go, she said, to one of the islands, and she never did and she died in another city and her ashes were brought back here.

[15]

A Bunch of Flowers
in a Glass

I said he wasn't going to die. He knew he was. When I said he wasn't he looked at me as he often did: as if there was something mysterious about me and as if, at the same time, I was a fool.

Marcel was about eighty. His life had been hard and perhaps about a third of it happy. He spent four months every year in the *alpage* with his cows. A third of his life at 1,700 metres. Surrounded by the metal of the mountains he knew a kind of peace. What I foolishly call happiness.

In the mountains he had two dogs, about forty cows and a bull. He liked it when friends came to visit him and he questioned them about news from below, about life in the village. He questioned them as one asks somebody about the latest episode in a TV serial.

His own life was up there – making cheeses, and imposing a precise but fragile daily order on the unceasing flow of days, nights, weathers, seasons, which passed the ledge where his chalet was. A ledge, near to the fire balls of lightning, and from which he could look down on a rainbow – as one looks down on the arch of a bridge one is crossing.

Up there, the question of solitude doesn't arise after a while – because one's naked. Naked one becomes aware of another kind of company. I don't know why this should be so. But it's a fact. Of course Marcel wasn't physically naked. On the contrary he didn't undress even to go to bed. Nevertheless after a week or two alone in the *alpage*, the soul goes naked, takes off its jacket – and one is no longer alone. This is what his eyes told.

The soul apart, there was the continual fear of mislaying an animal. His dogs knew the name of every cow but nevertheless a cow can easily get lost or break a leg. The laws of probability change up there. Sometimes the pine trees seem as if they've just stopped walking. There are nights when the Milky Way looks as close as a mosquito net. And there were August mornings when the handles of the metal wheelbarrow, in which he took the shit out of the milking stable, were frozen.

Marcel's hands were scoured, fissured, with swollen joints, and very warm. Calloused and at the same time sensitive. They were like certain old words that today are going out of use.

The last time I saw him was when I drove him home after we had seen the New Year in together. He was already waiting for next June to take his cows up to the *alpage* again. I told him it would happen. And he looked at me as sceptically as you look at a rockface from which an echo has come. Then he shook his head.

Last June I was on Marcel's mountain. There were no cows grazing, no bells, no dogs, but there were many wild flowers. Idly I began to pick a bunch. At this altitude the colours of flowers are more vivid than those of the same ones on the plain. Around the nearest peak I could see jackdaws flying. To the west I counted twenty parachutists in the sky. The rising air currents carry them up far higher than the edge from which they jump, and the site has recently become fabulous amongst *parapente* people.

I pushed open the door of Marcel's empty chalet. Two rooms – each one no larger than a railway compartment. On an impulse, I stuck the flowers in my fist into a glass, filled it with water, and put them on the table, where, at the end of the day, I used to drink coffee and he used to drink a bowl of milk. I didn't want to sit down on the bench now that he had gone. So I stood there, stood there, till I heard in the silence his voice shouting and swearing behind the cowbells of the herd in my head.

[16]

Two Recumbent Male Figures Wrestling on a Sidewalk

He has fought alongside guerrillas in the mountains many times in at least two continents. He's also an excellent cook. He will happily spend an entire day preparing an evening meal for friends. His name is Mohammed Brahim. Once when he and I were cutting up vegetables for a curry, he told me a story.

It began in 1947. Mohammed was thirteen years old. His voice had begun to break. Sometimes he spoke as gruffly as a man, at other times he spoke in a boy's falsetto. He couldn't control it. But he already had a man's decisiveness, he was already at risk like a man. I imagine the knowledge of that risk was in his eyes but I didn't know him then.

With independence, India was being partitioned. Twelve million people were on the roads, going in both directions, seeking safety. Mohammed's family had lived as Muslims for generations in India but now his elder brother decided to take the family to the newly created Pakistan.

The boys' mother refused to leave. Only mothers who are widows can become as immovable as she did. The rest of the family took the train for Lahore. In Delhi they learnt that the train would go no further: the fighting of the civil war was too dangerous. Everybody was lodged in a refugee camp. Mohammed's brother, who was a senior civil servant, telegraphed for a plane to come and rescue them. A whining man, begging for opium in the camp, caught Mohammed's attention. Misery importuning misery, he thought. Some youngsters pushed the man aside. Ay! Charsi! they mocked. Ay! Charsi! Opium-eater who lives in a cloud of smoke!

Finally the plane from Pakistan arrived. It was an ex-RAF Fokker. At the airport the two brothers were the last to embark. Every place was already taken.

You can fly in the cockpit with me, sir, the pilot shouted to his brother.

No, we're two, there's also Mohammed.

Then would you like me to tell somebody to get down, sir?

No, take Mohammed.

It was then that the thirteen year old revolted. He ran across the tarmac away from the plane.

Go, he shouted, go! I'm going to walk.

His brother, perhaps because he wanted to accompany his wife and small children, perhaps because he knew how obstinate and bone-headed Mohammed could be, climbed up into the plane and, standing by the still open door, said: All right, but take these! Whereupon he handed down a .22 single-barrel hunting gun, an ammunition belt and a 100-rupee note. Stay here and wait for the next plane, he added. Finally the Fokker took off.

Mohammed went to a restaurant and ordered in his gruff voice an elaborate dinner. The bill came to 10 rupees. Then he walked towards the Muslim quarter of Delhi. He could see in what direction to go, thanks to the minarets. He took the wide streets. Muslims in the city were being killed but with the rifle slung across his back he felt confident.

The following day he joined an immense column of refugees who were setting out to walk the several hundred kilometres to Lahore. The same afternoon, when the shadows were long, a portly middle-aged merchant walking behind Mohammed pointed at him and said to his companion that a youngster of his age should not be allowed arms. Let him at least be a gun-carrier, said the companion, like that we have less to carry.

The column slowly wound its way across the flat plain. Its pace was set by the oldest and most infirm, for they would have no hope of survival if left behind.

On the third day the column was attacked. Mohammed was among the first to see armed men coming across the irrigated fields towards them. He dropped to the ground, he took his time, he calmly remembered the deer-hunts on the family estate, and he shot down four of the marauders. After this he had the right, not only to carry his gun, but to fire it. He became one of the column's sentinels and marksmen.

As he strode up and down the column, he saw the opium-eater who, cut off from any supply of opium, was beginning to walk with a straighter back. He also noticed several young women and imagined their breasts brushing his cheek. One in particular he could not forget. She wore a tunic decorated with white flowers, small as stars. When the column halted, he loitered near her, but he was too shy to speak.

One midday when people were eating, he saw this woman walk into the mango grove beside the road. A man then followed her. Mohammed tracked the man, being careful to remain hidden. Next he saw the man lift the woman's *ghagra* and pull it over her head, and her struggling to push him away. When he saw this, instantly and without reflection, he raised his gun and fired.

Murderer! the woman screamed. Murderer!

The shot and the woman's cries brought men running from all directions. Mohammed fled across a field and found himself up against a stone wall. There he turned round to face the crowd.

If you take one step nearer, I'll shoot. When he said this it was in his falsetto voice, and his legs were trembling like a dog's a few seconds before an earthquake.

Suddenly the opium-eater was there, between the boy and his furious accusers. He no longer had a stick and he was standing upright.

Stop! he shouted. Stop!

The crowd lowered their voices and the man spoke quietly and gravely. You cannot start killing each other like this. Why are we making this journey, why are we fleeing? Because justice exists no more and because the stronger attack the weaker. The boy has to be given a trial. If you find him guilty, then you can punish him. He turned to Mohammed. Give me your gun. We cannot stop here. You'll march as a prisoner between two men.

That night a trial was held by firelight and the opium-eater was asked to be judge. What have you to say? he asked the accused. Before Mohammed had time to answer, the father of the young woman stepped forward into the firelight and said: My daughter has agreed that the man whom the boy killed was about to rape her. So be it, said Mohammed in his gruff voice.

After a few days the boy asked the Charsi his real name. Moosa, he replied, and they became friends. As the days went by, the opium-eater became the acknowledged leader of the column. It was he who decided the route, posted the sentries, settled disputes, sought help for the sick. When the caravan left Delhi it had numbered 30,000. Now it was half that number. Cholera broke out. Moosa organised the burying of the dead and such quarantine measures as were possible.

Wherever Moosa passed, he left behind him a kind of reassurance. It was a question of dignity. But, at night to Mohammed, he confessed his doubts: It will not be as we dream, when those of us who survive finally get there. Corrupt politicians have already ensconced themselves. They are waiting for us – waiting for us not as brothers but as our masters. They will use us.

At the frontier between the two newly divided states, the women wrapped themselves in their chadors. It was no longer dangerous for them to be seen veiled. Mohammed gazed for the last time at the woman with the tunic of white flowers. He had never spoken a word to her. Now the column numbered only 8,000.

Tonight, said Moosa to Mohammed, you will get your taxi and you will drive home. The journey is over for you.

There was a letter from his mother waiting for him. 'My boy, in this life we are sometimes forced to eat shit. If this happens, eat as you've been brought up to eat, and wash your hands afterwards.'

Seven months passed. One night, coming out of a restaurant in Lahore, Mohammed stumbled over a figure crouching on the sidewalk. He stopped in his tracks and he recognised Moosa. He bent down to speak to him. The Charsi gave no sign of recognition. Mohammed started to shake him. He called out his name: Moosa! Moosa! He shook him harder and harder until he lost his balance. They rolled together on the sidewalk trying to grasp each other. Moosa!

Overcome with anger and sorrow, Mohammed finally got to his feet, went home and wept. For three days he refused to see anybody. Then he took the decision to become a revolutionary: a decision he has never since renounced . . .

[17]

A Man Holding Up
a Horse's Bridle

In the winter he wore a green corduroy waistcoat over his pullover, but seldom a jacket. On his head, whether indoors or outdoors, he wore a small black beret, pulled discreetly over his eyes like a peaked cap. He was small and stocky, like his own work horse, a mare called Biche.

Biche was immortal, because when one mare was too old to work, he bought a young one, and, in turn, called her Biche.

Once he held up a bridle in front of my face.

Do you know what that means? he asked quietly.

Yes, I said, the mare's been taken away.

Fifteen years working together is a long time, he said.

He still held out the bridle in front of him. It was the only time I ever saw him make a theatrical gesture. The leather was encrusted with white from the salt of her sweat and the foam of her mouth.

Everything has its end, he finally said before hanging the bridle up on its wooden peg behind the stable door.

When I went to Paris last month, I put a photograph of him in my knapsack. I placed the photo carefully between the pages of a magazine with an article in it about post-industrial societies, so that it wouldn't get bent.

In the photo Théophile and I are facing each other in the kitchen of his farmhouse, which is bare and tiled like a dairy. It's winter, he has his beret on, and he's just about to pour some *gnole* into a little glass on the table. He's holding the bottle in his right hand, and in his left the stopper of the bottle between his finger and thumb.

It was many years ago, more than fifteen: my hair wasn't yet grey. I took the photo with me out of a kind of superstition. No, I took the photo with me as a kind of prayer. A prayer for his delivery. But Théophile was six weeks in the intensive-care unit before they let him die. I have come to mistrust most doctors because they no longer really love people.

The church was full and there were no places to sit down. The unnecessarily drawn-out suffering had made Théophile's death a jagged wound. Everyone felt this. Nobody among the three hundred people there smiled, even when shaking hands. He deserved better, they muttered.

You are assembled together, said the *Curé* to the standing villagers, to see him off on his last journey. Nothing in life is lost, the *Curé* went on, when the candles were lit on the coffin lid.

And suddenly I remembered. At that time Théophile and Jeanne had a dozen milking cows. The breed of l'Abondance. During the six winter months the animals stayed in the stable day and night. Once a week Théophile combed and, if necessary, cut their tails. And the hair he kept for stuffing mattresses.

They had no milking machine and so they milked by hand. Jeanne was the faster milker. My job each evening was to sweep out the stable, to give water to the mare – when she drank you could hear the water in her neck pouring as if from a pipe into a trough – to hose down the wheelbarrow after I'd emptied the shit on to the dung-heap, and to fetch, when needed, sacks of cattle feed.

These were kept in the *grenier*: a small wooden house apart from the main building so that its contents might be saved in case of fire. Every farm in the valley once had a *grenier*. They were built as solidly as galleons, but their thick doors were so small you had to bend to enter them.

The inside of Théophile's *grenier* was like his soul: a full, tidy depository of patience, energy and shrewdness. I would get the sack up on to my shoulder, and I would have to stoop to get through the doorway before pushing the door shut with my right boot and coming down the icy steps. Once I left the door open, and Théophile severely recited to me the list of possible enemies: the fox, the wild cat, the weasel, the boar, the mole, the crow, the stray dog, the field mouse, even the owl. Leaving the door open was an invitation to any or all of these to enter and destroy the wealth within.

Inside the stable, against the wall, was a wooden coffer into which I would empty the sacks. Théophile or Jeanne would then take the feed from the coffer in a pail and give it to the cows to munch each night whilst they were being milked. I remember the weight of the wooden lid and the firmness with which it shut. No enemy could get in there. He had made the coffer himself.

The young, Théophile maintained, took no risks any more, had no sense of patrimony! Thus, he indicated that he knew his sons would never farm the land he had inherited and worked.

Before emptying the sacks, I had to undo them. They were of stiff paper, sealed with a threaded white string. You needed a knife to cut the string. On a ledge above the coffer there was always an electric torch – in case of power failure – and a wooden pocket-knife.

You couldn't cut the string anywhere. There was only one place to nick it with the knife and then to pull out the whole unravelled length. If you cut elsewhere, you had to struggle, tear the paper, undo knots. But, cut at the right place, pulling the string was a joy like spinning a top. Indeed it unravelled so swiftly you could hear a hum.

In the dim light I sometimes found the right place, sometimes failed to. Théophile showed me a dozen times. He said nothing. He just nicked with the knife and pulled the string out before my eyes. A wordless demonstration.

Below the ledge where the torch and knife were kept, a large nail had been hammered into the stone wall. From this nail we hung the strings we pulled from the sacks. Like this he or Jeanne knew where to find a string when needed. A string, for instance, for tying a cow's tail to its left leg so it didn't flick your eyes when being milked.

Nothing in a life is lost, the *Curé* said.

[18]

Island of Sifnos

When I was sixteen years old a tram depot in London
– was it south of the river in New Cross? – made a
deep impression on me. First because of the number of
trams – there were a hundred or more – and, secondly,
because of how close together they stood to one another,
their lines having converged closer than they ever did
outside in the street. The trams stood there at night,
silent, empty, with only the width of a man's shoulders
between them. They were long, double-decker trams
with steep turning staircases at each end and their
large windows, aft and stern, were rounded. Before
it was light, one by one, the trams would leave the
depot for the four corners of the city, each following
the rails of its own route.

Unexpectedly the sight of the tram depot comes back
to me as we hurry along the quayside in the port of
Piraeus where the big Greek ships for the Aegean islands
dock side by side, their bulwarks almost touching.

The ship going to Sifnos is packed with half as
many passengers again as she was scheduled to take.
It is early Saturday morning, it is Whitsun week,
and it is already hot. On the open top deck every
square metre in the shade of the bridge or the
funnel or the lifeboats or the ventilators is already
occupied. By a companionway a smell of Greek
coffee wafts up from below. The crew all wear

sunglasses. The *meltem* isn't blowing and the sea is calm.

Within two hours the coast of the mainland is behind us and we begin to cross the circle of islands and to enter the Cyclades. The ship's population by now has settled down – like a hen in a basket when the journey to market is long, drowsy and its feathers spread. In the lounges below women fan themselves and their children as they sit in chairs – men passengers continually carry chairs from deck to deck – or as they lie in clusters on the floor.

Ah Baby! says a grandmother to a ship's officer in a white uniform, why have you done this to us? She has pulled her black skirt above her swollen knees, she has taken off her shoes and she is sitting on the carpet under a table. The company can't turn customers away, says the officer, and you're comfortable there, aren't you? Look at us, she says, all of us! and she indicates the sprawled bodies cushioning one another, as though these hundreds of bodies said all, and no more words were necessary for the whole voyage.

The beauty of the islands, as seen from the sea, is proverbial and difficult to describe. Blue. Crystalline. Aerial. (Towards the end of each day the sea horizon seems to move up to meet the sky.) Perhaps the most telling thing is to remember that it was here, in the

110

Aegean, that the first atomic theory of the universe was formulated. It fits. Every entity you look at is distinct, separate, and surrounded by limitless space.

On these islands, Aeschylus said, there's nothing but marble and goats and kings. In the mid-afternoon the ship puts us down on Sifnos. On Sifnos there are also olive trees, bitter laurel, vines, hibiscus, cacti.

Along a mule track, near a small cemetery where there is a white chapel, the size of a cart, with candles burning in it, three men are working together under an acacia tree and they are skinning two goats whose hind legs have been tied to one of the lower branches. Their dog, smelling the blood, whimpers. Tomorrow is the feast of Pentecost – the fiftieth day after Easter. In the churches sprigs of eucalyptus will be distributed and later the goats will be eaten.

Then suddenly as the light goes and I look over the cemetery towards the sea, I ask myself: What can flesh mean here? *Sarka* in Greek. All over the world women and men picture their bodies to themselves differently, for this picturing is influenced by the local terrain, the climate, and the surrounding natural risks. Like local crops, mental images of the flesh are regional. What is the Aegean image? It has, I think, little to do with scuba diving.

Flesh here is the only soft thing, the only substance

111

that can suggest a caress; everything else visible is sharp or mineral, shattered or gnarled. Flesh here is like the small exposed painted parts of those ikons which otherwise are entirely covered with unyielding and engraved metal. (You see them in every church.) Flesh is simultaneously wound and healing. Look at us, said the old woman to the ship's officer, all of us!

Consequently the body is aware of a cruelty even before it is aware of pleasure, for its own existence is cruel. Thus for everybody, not just philosophers and theologians, the physical lurches constantly towards the metaphysical. The lurch doesn't require words, a glance is sufficient. There's nobody here who isn't an expert in longing, in the long drawn-out desire for a life a fraction less cruel. And oddly, this co-exists with the beauty and is part of it.

All those sculptures, stolen from Greece and now in foreign museums, are strangely unsensual and that's one reason why they belong here. The sensual in art is some-how a celebration of a complicity, a continuity between body and nature. Here no such complicity exists. The famous 'ideal' which the classical sculptors sought was, in fact, a consolation for the body's loneliness. All those sculptures, it seems to me now, were messengers of a very controlled longing without end.

And earlier – four thousand years before – the

Cycladic sculptures from these islands were worked in such a way that their marble looks more like some gentle, kneaded substance, and the figures of the men and women, naked in an indifferent world, like loaves of unleavened bread.

Night has fallen and the cicadas have started up. For the first time this year, our landlady tells us, they won't stop, they'll go on all summer!

'I shall mourn always,' wrote Odysseus Elytis who speaks for the crowd on the boat and the shepherd on the mountain and the men under the acacia tree and us sitting at a table drinking wine, 'I shall mourn always – do you hear me? – for you alone in Paradise.'

A longing without end.

On the number 23 tram I used to sit on the top deck and, if possible, at the very back from where I could hear the sparks spluttering from the overhead electric wire. And there I sometimes dreamt, as the tram followed its lines, of islands, of women in the sun, of the sea, and I didn't know yet the marvellous poetry of Odysseus Elytis.

'Until at last I felt – and let them call me crazy – that out of nothing is born our Paradise.'

[19]

A Painting of an
Electric Light Bulb

Rostia invited me to his studio. It's the first time in his life he has had a studio. A few years ago he used to paint, when it was sunny, in the shell of a ruined outhouse somewhere in the north of the capital. The new studio, allotted to him by the city of Paris, is in Chatenay Malabry. He was born in Prague in 1954.

I first met Rostia in the early eighties when he was selling crêpes at night on the Blvd. St Michel. He spoke French with an accent like the River Danube. And he looked like a man who had just come out of a conscript army in which he had served quite a while. Glad to be free. Single. Not an officer, not even a corporal. A bit lost in civilian life. In fact he was never in the Czech or any other army. But the long struggle of growing up, surviving, refusing, emigration, had been for Rostia like being in the army. Manoeuvre after manoeuvre. And during that time all he had dreamt was to be on leave – which meant painting furiously on whatever he could lay his hands.

His pictures were rubbishy, a bit subversive and memorable because of their awkwardness. Rubbishy in that they were badly presented and painted with whatever was at hand. Subversive in that, as you went on looking at their abstract confetti of colours, you suddenly spotted a dog or a grinning kid hidden within them. And awkward in that they assumed no manners that they didn't have. They were just themselves, like the handle of a hammer painted red so it doesn't get lost.

I liked their hooligan company and his. We used to drink beer together, pushing our caps to the back of our heads and sticking out our legs as if wearing dungarees. When we could find the right words in translation we told one another jokes.

In those days, women didn't treat Rostia as well as he deserved. They pictured him as a kind of bear on a circus poster. And he didn't make things better because, like many men who spend years in the army, he tended to be a bit paranoic. Sometimes it was difficult to guess what he was going on about.

Drinking our beer together we never once mentioned Hegel or Lukacs or Paul Klee or Dvořák. We took a lot for granted and I knew that, if we should get into a fight in one of the bars, I could count on him. His bear size and his uncannily observant eye would help.

Once, walking back over the bridges, each with an arm round the other's shoulder, we reminisced about the wooden doorways of Prague, with doors as large as lorries. And for a moment the Seine became the Vltava for us both.

When I arrived at the studio in Chatenay Malabry, Rostia's daughter, Andrea, was in her cot about to go to sleep. She's almost two. Rostia no longer sells crêpes but

116

works part-time drawing plans in an architect's office. He and Laurence sleep on the loggia overlooking the studio space, and we ate at the table beside their bed.

He wanted me to look at his recent paintings. He went down to the studio floor and stapled the unstretched canvases, one after another, on to the wall. When there was a large one, Laurence helped him, and as I watched from above, I saw her, small, nimble, balancing like a trick cyclist beside the circus bear.

The pictures were no longer hooligan. They were still awkward, but they were absolutely sure of themselves. The subject was always the same. Metal lampshades hanging on their flexes with electric light bulbs. But on each canvas the arena of their light was a different but vast landscape. A landscape where? Not mid-European, not French, not Celtic. Just a stretch of land somewhere on the surface of the earth, lit by two, three, or four bulbs, illuminating together like a family. The more I looked, the more surely I knew they were remarkable, and the more pensive I became. Sometimes I read in a newspaper that I am (or was) one of the most influential writers about art in the English language. Yet I know nobody in the art trade in Paris or anywhere else. Nobody.

Neither I nor Rostia would get past any art expert's first secretary. And, if by any chance we did, if we

117

actually met a dealer, he'd look at us as if we were out of some village circus. I knew the canvases I was looking at deserved to be framed, exhibited, sold, hung in houses. And yet there was nothing I could do about it.

Rostia interrupted my thoughts: What's up? You don't like the dark one?

Let's drink to Andrea! I said, but I couldn't get rid of a nagging frustration. I wanted to see those furiously painted canvases out in the world, relying on their own authority.

We started talking about mixing colours – Rostia uses both oil and tempera – and how much cheaper it is than buying tubes. He held up a tin of cadmium yellow. Then he opened a bottle of linseed oil and he handed it to me as if he expected me to take a swig. Did he know what the effect would be?

I sniffed it and I forgot my frustrations. I was twelve years old again. I was with my first box of oil paints and my first palette the size of a school exercise book. I was handling the tubes with their exotic, distant names. Indian Red. Naples Yellow. Burnt Umber. Raw Sienna. And the mysteriously named Flake White – suggesting snowflakes in a blizzard.

The smell of that oil (the same oil with which one softens putty when putting in a window pane) took

118

me back half a century to a promise. The promise of painting and painting, the promise of doing it every day of your life, and thinking about nothing else until you are dead!

[20]

A Girl Like Antigone

It measures, I guess, 80 cm x 200 cm. More or less the size of what you sleep on if you take a railway couchette. Not made of oak, but probably of pearwood which has a warmer colour. On it is a table lamp, also in wood, of a vaguely Bauhaus design, perhaps dating from the twenties, when the family first moved into the apartment. A modest, functional lamp looking almost hand-made, but insistent in its promise of modernity, a promise which she never for a moment believed in.

The table is in the room where she worked and slept when she was at home. In her vagrant life she must have spent more time reading and writing at this table than at any other.

I've never met anybody who knew her. I've looked at many photographs. I drew a portrait of her from a photograph. Perhaps this is why I have the strange impression that a long time ago I set eyes on her. I can recall the mixed feelings she inspired in me: a physical antipathy, a sense of my own inadequacy, a certain exhilaration at the opportunity she appeared to offer of loving. A love, as in Plato's *Timée*, whose mother is Poverty. She was disconcerting, no question.

I saw the table in Paris last week. Behind it are some bookshelves and on them some of the books she read. The room is long and narrow like the table. When she sat behind it, the door was on her left. The door gives

121

on to a corridor: opposite was her father's consulting room. When she walked down the corridor towards the front door she would have passed the waiting room on her left. The sick, or those who feared they were sick, were immediately outside her door. She could have heard her father saying goodbye to each patient and then greeting the next one:

Bonjour Madame, sit down and tell me how you are.

On the right of her table is the window. A large one facing north. The apartment is on the sixth floor and the Rue Auguste Comte is on a slight hill, so there is a view over Paris, from the Luxembourg Gardens, just below, to beyond the Sacré Coeur. You stand at the window, you open it, you lean against the railing of the balcony on which no more than four pigeons could land, and you fly in imagination over the roofs and history. It's the exact height for flights of the imagination: the height of birds flying to the far edge of the city, to the walls, where the present ends and another epoch begins. In no other city in the world are such flights so elegant. She loved the view from the window, and she was deeply suspicious of its privilege.

'There is a natural alliance between truth and affliction, because both of them are mute supplicants, eternally condemned to stand speechless in our presence.'

She began writing on the table when she was at the

122

Lycée Henri IV, preparing to enter the École normale. She had by then already begun the third notebook of the journal she was going to keep all her life.

She died in August 1943 in a sanatorium in Ashford, Kent. The coroner's report gave the cause of death as 'cardial failure due to myocardial degeneration of the heart muscles due to starvation and pulmonary tuberculosis'. She was thirty-four years old. The verdict was suicide, because she stopped eating.

What is special about her handwriting? It is patient, conscientious – like a student's – but each letter – whether Roman or Greek – has been formed (almost drawn) like an Egyptian hieroglyph, so much did she want each letter of each word to have a body.

She travelled to many places and she wrote wherever she was lodged, yet everything she wrote might have been written here. Whenever she had a pen in her hand, she returned in her mind to this table in order to begin thinking. Then she forgot the table.

If you ask me how I know this, I have no answer.

I sat at the table and read a poem which had marked a turning point in her life. In her hieroglyphic handwriting she had copied out the poem in English and learnt it by heart. At moments when she was overcome by despair or the pain of a migraine behind her eyes, she used to recite it out loud, like a prayer.

On one such occasion, whilst reading it, she felt the physical presence of Christ and was astonished. Visions, like the miracles of the New Testament, put her off; she found them too easy. '. . . in this sudden hold that Christ had on me, neither my imagination nor my senses played any part; I simply felt, across the pain, the presence of love, similar to that which one can read in a smile on a loved face.'

Fifty years later, as I read the sonnet by George Herbert, the poem became a place, a dwelling. There was nobody in it. Inside it was shaped like a stone beehive. There are tombs and shelters like this in the Sahara. I have read many poems in my life but I had never before *visited* one. The words were the stones of a habitation which surrounded me.

In the street below, above the entrance to the apartment block (today you need to tap a code to get in), there is a plaque which reads: 'Simone Weil, philosopher, lived here between 1926 and 1942.'

[21]

A Friend Talking

(for Guzine)

Sometimes it seems that, like an ancient Greek, I write mostly about the dead and death. If this is so, I can only add that it is done with a sense of urgency which belongs uniquely to life.

Abidine Dino lived with his beloved Guzine on the ninth floor of an HLM in one of those artists' studios built, at a certain period, by the city of Paris for painters. They were happy there, but if you added all the space of the studio and its closets together, it would come to no more than the space available for the passengers in a long-distance bus. Translations, poems, letters, sculptures, drawings, mathematical models, raki, almonds covered with cocoa, cassettes of Guzine's radio programmes in Turkish, elegant clothes (both of them in their different ways dressed as impeccable stylists), newspapers, pebbles, canvases, water-colours, photos – everything was packed in. And whenever I visited, I came away with my head full of the space of vast landscapes, even of Greater Anatolia – in such a way did Abidine and Guzine drive the coach in which they lived.

This week Abidine Dino died in the Paris hospital of Villejuif. He died three days after he lost his voice and could speak no more.

A week ago almost the last thing Abidine told me was: Don't exaggerate in your new book. You don't need extravagance. Stay realist. He was a realist about his cancer. He knew how grave it was. But the adjective he used about his state of health was the adjective you might use about a shoe that pinched and which you had to walk a long way in.

Any image which comes to me about him when alive inevitably includes roads, caravanserai, voyages. He had a traveller's vigilance. As Saadi the Persian wrote:

He who sleeps on the Road will lose either
his hat or his head.

In the small book-alcove of the studio, or before the portable easel which he folded up at night, Abidine continually travelled. He painted women who became planets. He drew the pain of hospital patients as with the recording needle of a seismograph. Not long ago he gave me photocopies of some drawings he had made about the tortured. (Like many of his friends he had been in prison in Turkey.) Look at them, he said, as he accompanied me to the lift on the ninth floor, and one day some words from far away may come to you. Perhaps just one word or two. That will be enough. He painted flowers – their throats, their Bosporus passages to love. This summer, at the age of eighty, whilst staying in a *yali*, a house on the real Bosporus, he painted a white door with a mysterious sign on it. A white door which was not in the *yali* but elsewhere.

On the night of his death, I woke up in the small hours of the morning. I woke up to the knowledge that he had died, and I prayed for him. I tried to become a lens in a kind of telescope so that an angel somewhere might see Abidine a little better as he accompanied him. Maybe not better. Simply a little more. Then I found myself face to face with a sheet of white paper, so full of light there was no place there for any orphaned colour.

Later I fell asleep, in no way anguished. Early next morning Selcuk, our mutual friend, telephoned to tell me we had lost Abidine. (He had died in the hospital about two hours before I woke up.)

This time I wept, choking with the grief of a dog. Grief is animal. The ancient Greeks knew that.

Men often say, referring to a noble man's death, that a light has gone out. It is a cliché, yet how better to describe the dusk afterwards? The white paper I saw became charcoal – black, and charcoal is the colour of absence.

Absence? The sign Abidine painted on the white door this summer reminded me of another series of drawings and paintings he made during the last months. They were of crowds. Images of countless faces, each

129

person distinct, but together in their energy similar to molecules. The images, however, were neither sinister nor symbolic. When he first showed them to me I thought this multitude of faces were like the letters of an undeciphered writing. They were mysteriously fluent and beautiful. Now I ask myself whether Abidine had not travelled again, whether these were not already pictures of the dead?

And at this moment he answers the questions, for suddenly I remember him quoting Ibn al Arabi: 'I see and note the faces of all who have lived and will one day live, from Adam until the end of time . . .'

[22]

Two Men Beside
a Cow's Head

On New Year's Day Louis had called me to help him with Blanquette who was calving. He had been into the stable twenty times since morning to feel with his fist if the end of Blanquette's tail was soft and not rigid. Their tails go soft just before birth. Outside everything was white and in the branches of the pear trees there were parcels of snow as large as sacks. Blanquette's waters had broken but only one hind foot had emerged.

Louis put his arm in to search for the second leg; he found it bent double but it was so slippery inside he couldn't turn it. *Nom de Dieu!* he said.

I had taken a stick and was pressing it with all my weight against Blanquette's spine, near the shoulders. The pressure makes the basin untighten. Meanwhile Louis, his arm up to his armpit inside her, tried again to turn the calf's leg. Turned it! he hissed.

Then he had slipped a rope over one of the feet. Slowly, as we hauled, the legs came out. They were white, smeared with brownish pink, the smears being partly the colour of the hair, and partly the colour of blood, the sweet blood of that hard passage we all forget.

The calf slipped through our arms on to the straw. Its eyes were shut. Louis threw a bucket of cold water over its face. It sighed once. A single breath. It was a male. His white tongue lolled out of the corner of his mouth. Louis held the mouth open and I breathed into the throat. He massaged the heart. We poured *gnole* on to the tongue. Took too long! said Louis.

Louis calculated that beneath the linden tree the earth wouldn't be frozen very hard, for the slope faces south. He tramped through the snow with a pick and shovel. I dragged the calf over the ground with the rope still attached to his leg. He slipped into the pit, his inert body naturally folding itself to take up as little space as it had inside Blanquette. The calf's muzzle was pointing to the sky.

Louis had bent down, saying: Never knew what life was! Then he had turned the calf's head on to its side, so that, when he threw in the first spadeful of earth, it would not hit the muzzle.

The calf who died on New Year's Day was a bad omen we hadn't quite forgotten.

Now the Duchess had colic. She had probably eaten some bad grass. She was lying down, she was refusing to eat, she didn't move her jaws. With their four stomachs cows are fragile. Digestion is their Achilles' heel – if anything about this docile, nimble animal-species can be compared with Achilles!

Louis felt the temperature of the Duchess's ears, looked at her eyes, clasped her tail. The veterinary surgeon is expensive. We decided to administer the family medicine for a cow with colic.

He went to fetch some *gnole* and I meanwhile ground some coffee beans. Then I found an old plastic vinegar bottle, washed it out, poured into it two cupfuls of *gnole* and topped it up with strong fresh black coffee. I tasted the mixture to make sure it wasn't too hot. A feeling of urgency prevented us from patiently waiting for the coffee to cool.

We returned to the stable with the bottle and Louis shortened the rope by which Duchess was attached to a ring in the wall, and he put her huge head under his arm. With his other hand he tried to force her mouth open. When cows are confused, they play stupid. The Duchess wouldn't open. Louis pressed with his fingers against her pale-pink gums, he tugged at her immense lip. Finally she opened. I poured from the vinegar bottle into her gullet. She swallowed the coffee and *gnole*. Then, with her uncarnivorous teeth, she shut up like a small whale – but delicately, crushing no finger.

All we can do now is wait till tomorrow, Louis said.

[23]

A Man Baring His Chest

A crowd. So large that one can't imagine it, even when one is part of it. A crowd in which all that the past has left is bursting out, searching, cheating, achieving, hoping, waiting, despairing for a future.

The crowd is there because of the market. Getting richer. Getting poorer with the hope of getting a fraction richer later. The market has nothing to do with the wealthy. Here a voice and a glance of the eyes can still make a difference. Everything glistens because it may be a bargain. Everything sold is a little gain because it has been sold.

Octopus, sparking plugs, hair combs, pomegranates, cassettes, pig bladders, celery, old ribbons, rings, jeans, new shoes, old shoes, exhaust pipes, samovars, bread, lamb meat, black peppers, sheets, pillowcases, nappies, irons, perfumes, chicken liver, almonds, crash helmets, figs, wooden spoons, cameras . . .

I'm looking for a whet stone to sharpen knives with. (Simple pleasures: to gather flowers in the morning and bring them into a room and place them in a vase. To cut with a sharp knife. To splash cold water on the face after sleep. To receive a letter from a loved one.) I go from stall to stall. Nobody is beautiful. Everyone is second-hand and powdered with dust. Everyone has at least one joke. And some have a pride which outdoes beauty.

137

It's difficult to walk because the crowd is so tightly packed. Each person has to proceed like a trickle of water finding his way between pebbles. And for the others he is a pebble.

One can read about demographic curves in the newspapers, but in such a crowd the energy of procreation, as patient and violent as the current of a great river, is a warmth, a radiation felt on the back of the hands and a smell which mixes with all the others of *mazout*, car fumes, cement dust, fish, cinnamon, shit, burning plastic, iodine, honey and vinegar. Life insisting on itself in the Omonia district of Athens just below the Acropolis.

At last I find a whet stone, spit on it and try it out on a knife. The vendor, unsmiling, nods his head, for he knows that I am now almost morally obliged to buy it and I haven't yet proposed a price. The noise of a whet stone running along a blade is swift and yet granular. Like a snake crossing sand.

How much?

Six hundred.

Five.

He wraps up the stone in a newspaper. And it was at that moment that I saw the blind man. He had a white stick and was wearing an unbuttoned shirt. He was moving through the crowd with more ease than anybody else. His face had a concentrated expression.

The tool vendor gives me a five hundred note as change for a thousand, and I place it in the blind man's open hand. He had paused, waiting for me to do this. He is blind in such a way that his eyes (he wears no glasses) are permanently shut. He must be in his forties. Still holding the money, he pulls open his shirt to reveal his chest. Pale in colour, ribs distinctly visible. Beneath his left nipple there is a piece of lint stuck to his skin with adhesive tape.

Then I see, pinned to the inside of his shirt, a brooch. A part of me immediately reasons that the brooch, when his shirt is hanging normally, may be the cause of the sore which the little dressing covers. Another part of me is amazed to see a painted crucifixion on the medallion of the brooch. The cross is very near – one could put out one's hand to touch its wood, as in the large picture painted by Velázquez when he was thirty-one years old.

The blind beggar holds his shirt open and waits to make sure I've seen the miniature. I think he can hear me looking at it.

The eye is the lamp of the body, he says as he begins his ritual recitation. If your eyes are good, your whole body will be full of light. But if your eyes are bad, your whole body will be full of darkness. If then the light within you is darkness, how great is that darkness.

I found the passage in the Gospel of St Matthew.

[24]

A House in the
Sabine Mountains

About her I know for certain only two things. The first is that she's the mother of my friend Riccardo and the second I'll tell you at the end.

A dust road runs along the crest of a long undulating hill. Sometimes the slopes on either side are steep enough for the hill to merit almost the name of a mountain. The road runs through olive groves and leads past two or three small houses until it reaches the last one, which is where Riccardo's mother was born in the 1920's at about the time Mussolini took over the country, and there it stops because the hill stops. You stand there and it's like standing on the prow of a high ship and you look over the sea of hills and valleys, stretching to the horizon.

To the north there's a small town built on a hill-top like a fortress. In its town hall thousands of documents are stacked in piles, recording marriages, deals, litigations, deaths, transfers of property, the birth of children legitimate and illegitimate, fines paid, years of military service completed, criminal charges, debts paid and unpaid, yet, as the years pass and the recorded events recede, the ferocious choices made on these occasions are forgotten and only the recurring names – since all the families were related – only the recurring names still murmur like the sea.

The road was always full of surprises because the

baked soil, the chips of stone, the grasses, the thistles, the lizards, the fossils of sea shells, the wild chicory, the thunder when there was a storm, the silver of the wet olive leaves afterwards, and, next day, the stillness of the early afternoon heat around your ankles as you walked along it, these events were as endless as childhood itself, and none of them could be kept in place for long, since it would wriggle out at the far end and be back the next day. To maintain the minimal order among these hills required the work of generations.

Today the olive trees are still in their rows. A few, near the houses, have been pruned so that their branches follow a logic like the fingers of an extended hand. But some of the trees grow unchecked and undergrowth is burying the terraces. The first houses along the road have been done up and painted in unheard-of colours: the colours invented after the discovery of polyesters. Nobody lives on the road any more. The grown-up children of the last inhabitants come for weekends, do what they can, rest a little, pick the figs when they are ripe. But the endless work has stopped. And the last house is deserted.

Riccardo's mother left it when she got married, as did the other children. The grandparents stayed on until they died. It has been empty for forty years.

In one of its thick walls there is an oven for baking

bread. The cellar below was a stable for the donkey and the horse. In the downstairs room there's a concrete sink and a cooking stove to be heated by embers taken from the fire. Every day, every year, during mealtimes, this confined room was crowded and noisy. A staircase, almost as steep as a ladder, leads up to the parents' bedroom. From there you jump down into an annexe like a ship's fo'c'sle where the ship's crew sleep. This fo'c'sle was the children's and everybody else's bedroom. To be indoors in this house was to be close to others. If you wanted solitude you went out and climbed down to one of the rocks.

As soon as you woke, you slid down the steep staircase and you ran out to the prow to look across the valleys. Each day was the same and was different. When you woke up late, and you went out there, you heard the horse behind you blowing out his breath and making his big lips quiver.

Since some time the weight of the house's roof has forced the long walls to cave outwards. The beams sag. The damp, which nags old mortar to dust, has entered everywhere. The doors no longer hang true. The house is saveable but to restore it will cost money. From time to time the family talks about it: all the children need to agree. Would any of them ever live there? When? How to win a lottery to get enough money?

Meanwhile, eighteen months ago, Riccardo's mother made a decision of her own. She obtained a jasmine plant. She went to the house at the end of the road, the house in which she was born, and in the earth against the southern wall by the side of the door, she planted the jasmine plant and tied it carefully with raffia to a stick, so it might resist the wind and, when there are storms, the rain.

It's doing well and is 50 centimetres high. This is the second thing I know for sure.

[25]

Two Cats in a Basket

A chimney goes up through the centre of his house. Every winter – except for the few years when the farmhouse was unoccupied, this was before the man lived there – the chimney has been heated by a fire in the kitchen, a fire to which the chimney gives a draught.

The stoves which held the fire have perhaps changed, but nothing else. The mason who planned and constructed the chimney would be as proud of his work today as he must have been when he fixed a pine to the roof to announce that the building of the house was finished. That evening there was a *fête* in the village and everyone drank to the new home. Over the front door, made of panels of pearwood, the mason carved his initials and the date in stone: C.J. 1883.

Behind the stove now, in 1993, there's a shopping basket, half full of kindling wood. The basket was made by another mason. He built the walls of the escarpment along the *route nationale* at the other end of the village, and when he was old and his wife had died, he liked to plait baskets for his friends. On top of the kindling wood in the basket behind the stove lie two sleeping cats. They look like a calendar picture for the month of January. They lie, heads touching and their forelegs around each other. A mother and a daughter. Occasionally one of them moves and licks the other's face.

A man is sitting in a chair beside the stove, idly

watching the two cats in the basket. Animals sleep with members of their family but seldom with their mates. Human rhythms are different, accompanied by different fears. Yet the mutual pleasure of the cats behind the stove communicates a kind of happiness which is familiar.

In the spring when the two cats are on heat and after they've been mounted and the tom-cats have left, in the spring they lie on their backs in the dust and their paws jerk and their heads roll from side to side, as they stretch to make themselves longer.

Whilst the man alone in his kitchen on a winter's night gazes dreamily at the basket made by Jean-Marie, he thinks that, just as cats have no need to sleep with their lovers, the gender of animals, unlike that of humans, doesn't suggest a division or a separation into two parts of something which was once one. It's only men and women who long for a lost unity. The cats are dreaming of their own languor and warmth behind the stove. And when one licks the other, it's as if she's licking a part of herself.

He remembers a story that talks of this.

In the beginning was a single lump of clay with four arms and four legs. One day God decided to cut it into two equal parts. Afterwards he had to sew up the two new bodies with string where he'd cut them. He had a ball of string with him. And he bit it with his teeth into what he thought were two equal lengths. And there he made a mistake. One was longer than the other. With the short string he sewed up one body but there wasn't enough to sew right the way round. With the other one there was too much string, so he made a knot and let one end dangle!

The man by the stove smiles because it's so easy to recognise himself in the story. But with the two cats nobody made a mistake. He puts a log into the fire. Outside it is cold. Mineral cold. He tells himself another version of the beginning.

God decided to give men free will. As soon as there was such a thing as free will, the natural laws of necessity – all the laws of cause and effect – were called into play. Every story ever told by men or women is in part a protest against the indifference of those laws.

The orange-and-white mother cat puts her hind leg over the black daughter cat.

Life became hard and cruel. So cruel that men, and particularly women, could not bring themselves to wish life on to another. It was better not to be born, and better, they said, not to give birth, they would stop. It was then that God had to invent all the acts that promise sexual pleasure. One by one he invented them. And since that time, when making love women and men pardon this life and glimpse another . . .

The man's head nods, his chin touches his chest as he drifts into sleep and the chimney draws the fire.

[26]

A Young Woman
Wearing a Chapka

Olga. I call you that because I don't know your name. Nor your age. My guess is nineteen. All I know for certain about your origins is that you were in Moscow on the evening of Sunday, October the 3rd, 1993.

You have a head wound with a bandage. The bandage is not very visible because you're wearing a chapka which you took from a soldier who had just been killed. You also took his fur jacket and army belt which you are wearing. I guess you took his gun too, but it's not in the photograph. You took them as if he had bequeathed them to you. He was fighting on your side. Probably he was one of the Cossacks who crossed the lines to join Routskoy.

You were wounded when you and several thousand others, barely armed, tried to take the television building of Ostakino. Now you have come back to defend the parliament in the White House: the parliament that has been under siege for twelve days because it is said to be a danger for democracy.

You are pale, thoughtful. Your eyes have an expression that comes from looking intently at something which is neither close-at-hand nor distant. You are looking at what-might-have-been a few hours ago. Now you know that the Omons, the Forces of Order, are shooting to kill. It has been decided in the Kremlin that

153

more deaths are acceptable. Out there their fire-power is shattering.

You know this and you came back to defend the White House, since what is at stake is more than either defeat or victory. Now that they want deaths, they are bound to win.

At stake is your delicacy and, for example, the belt you're wearing. It could have been from your father's uniform, even your grandfather's.

It is not only the rouble which has lost its value a thousandfold during the last two years. Everything once lived has lost its value. Everything has become junk for sale. Each day in the streets you have seen people selling treasures, once close to their hearts, in order to buy sugar or a pair of boots for the winter. All the sacrifices of three generations are now being sacrificed on the altar of the Free Market. And, once sacrificed, instantly spent so that nothing remains. Nothing.

With your delicacy you came to protect against that nothing.

The news headlines pretended you were nostalgic for communism and were a threat to democracy. According to them you took your country to the brink of civil war, Olga, then, fortunately, the people were saved by Yeltsin, backed by the statesmen of the West.

The memory of the people, however, is not as short

as the dealers assumed. And this is already visible in your face. It is hard to decide whether you are a child or a grandmother. (At historic moments, two, three, even four generations are sometimes compressed and co-exist within the lived experience of a single hour. Those who believe that history is finished have forgotten this.) It is hard to know whether you came to defend the White House because you have classmates who have emigrated to become prostitutes in Hamburg or Zurich, or because you remember losing a husband fifty years ago in the battle of Stalingrad. This too is part of your delicacy.

The dealers of the Free Market and their corollary, the Mafia, assume they now have the world in their pocket. They have. But to maintain their confidence they have to change the meaning of all the words used in languages to explain or praise or give value to life: every word, according to them now, is the servant of profit. And so they have become dumb. Or, rather, they can no longer speak any truth. Their language is too withered for that. As a consequence they have also lost the faculty of memory. A loss which one day will be fatal.

Tomorrow, Olga, a friend will change your bandage.

Of the photograph I make this verbal photocopy so that some who missed the photo in the French press on Tuesday, October the 5th, 1993, will see you.

155

[27]

Men and Women
Sitting at a
Table and Eating

Two lunches during my lifetime, and in memory they are filed side by side. The two occasions may seem to be in contrast, yet I doubt whether this is why my imagination persists in placing them together. Anyway, the two photocopies are for ever on the same page.

The first was at Maxim's in Paris. I was invited to the legendary restaurant by some Russian friends who worked for the theatre. I had some difficulty in being admitted to the dining-room because I wasn't wearing a tie. The entrance barman agreed to lend me one which he asked me to select from a drawer. There was a choice of colours – all of them sombre. For a fraction of a second, standing before a mirror, I wondered whether I would remember how to tie the knot.

Finally I joined the others. We were about twenty, and we sat at a long table as in a refectory. The other smaller tables, already occupied, were far from us, placed further into the somewhat mysterious décor of the restaurant. Mysterious in the same way as a stage in a full theatre is mysterious before the first words have been spoken. Downstage we were alone.

We started to talk and to drink from our glasses and to eat – with the impression of eating little, spared any burden of consuming! Soon we forgot where we were, and I had the sensation of sailing on a river in a long boat. Between each of us at the table there was

157

an invisible oarsman, almost continually there, almost continually rowing, yet invisible, for he performed his duties only when our glances were elsewhere. These oarsmen were the waiters and they rowed by foreseeing, arranging and serving our every last wish.

I ate sole fourrée with prawns and mushrooms. The sauce over the fish was the colour of a milky opal and the marigold carrots were sliced as thin as wafers.

We were the dead gliding harmoniously, unhindered, downstream and across the river to our funeral pyre. We were in fact alive, tasting, swallowing, wiping our mouths, remaining sober, laughing, enjoying ourselves, trying to remember, telling stories, but we were also *foutus* (everything reassuringly demonstrated it) and we were in the hands of the ferrymen.

Naturally in these circumstances the meal went on longer than anybody noticed, we found ourselves late and in a hurry and so were obliged to take a taxi. The driver was a woman.

So you lunched at Maxim's? she asked smiling. I've never been there but if the chance comes it's something you should do once in a lifetime, no? she said.

The second meal was in the small Galician town of Betanzos on the north-west tip of Spain. On the Day of Ascension in mid-August. It also happened to be

158

market day, and on market days in Betanzos a canteen on a hill, a little outside the town where the animal pens are, opens for lunch, always offering the same dish.

It is hot, the selling is over. The unsold cattle are being herded back into their lorries. A man of my age in a white suit, which would be worthy of a count, is loading his old Peugeot with cages of unsold chicks. Behind the driving seat there are packaged eggs and the floor of the car is covered with tiny brown feathers. Now it's time to eat. Dressed as he is today in his ivory suit and silver tie, the chicken-count could be admitted to Maxim's.

I follow him into the canteen: a concrete hangar with a corrugated roof, windows high up on the wall, and on the asphalt floor, rows of narrow wooden tables made of three planks, the width of three hands. Two hundred or more people are already sitting on the benches eating. Each one of them, like the chicken-count, has dressed for the occasion.

Ascension Day is the sexiest of the religious fiestas. A little like a heavenly wedding, but lighter than a marriage. So, a new comb in the hair. Clean jeans. White socks. Ribbons for the very young children. Wear the new cap for the first time. Put on your angel shoes.

Every year since a century ago, the town of Betanzos

159

releases at midnight a multi-coloured air balloon into the sky, and, gas-jets burning, it ascends as the Madonna once did. And every year the thousands of spectators waiting gasp as they follow it and its passengers with their eyes, as if their breath might help them on their way.

In the canteen now, along the wall opposite the entrance, burn braziers of flaming wood. On each fire is balanced a massive copper cauldron of water which has been simmering since dawn. The cooks are women dressed in peasant black, and they stand behind the cauldrons. Whenever more food is needed, one of them bends over the steaming water and forks out another cooked octopus.

The creatures are big, the size of the largest sun-flowers. Before being put into the cauldron they were smashed against rocks to make their flesh tender. Then they were lowered into the water three times before being left to cook in it. The third time they turned reddish.

A woman in black settles a cooked octopus on a wooden worktable. It glistens there, no longer reddish but phosphorescent – with the colours of gas-jets – green, white, violet. She cuts it with a pair of secateurs into round slices. The slices are about the size of signet rings. Sprinkled with salt, vinegar, oil, cayenne, and served on round wooden plates, these rings are the feast.

The wooden plates are shared. You spear the jewel you've chosen with a wooden toothpick and you eat it with Galician bread which has kept the secret of yeast.

Each of the narrow tables has its wooden plates, its little glasses of toothpicks, its piles of bread and its white china bowls for drinking the local rosé wine. The rings of octopus taste of the sea and of sailors' lips.

Behind me some cattle dealers with their hats pushed back – they wear their hats so they can be spotted in the crowd from a distance – drink from their white bowls and look triumphant. So does a four year old in a black velvet dress sitting at the next table. So do the worker's family on holiday from Madrid. A quiet, not exuberant, almost suppressed triumph – like a joke one is trying to keep to oneself. This keeping of a secret is most clearly expressed on the face of an old man opposite me telling a story to an old woman.

In the heat, which would stop any dog from barking, I look around the canteen, china bowl to my lips, rosé and octopus in my mouth, and I wonder: What's the triumph about? And an answer comes.

Everyone has dressed up and climbed the hill

to the canteen. Another year has passed, another summer, they have all come here, they are all still here on this earth, each with a toothpick for the feast!

$$\left[\; 28\; \right]$$

Room 19

It was called the Hotel du Printemps and was in the 14th arrondissement. The entrance with a reception desk was no wider than a corridor. Room number 19 was on the third floor. A steep staircase with no lift. Sven and I climbed slowly up to his room. He had arrived in Paris the day before and we had been friends for forty years.

Room 19 was small with a window which gave on to a deep narrow yard. The light's better in the toilet, said Sven. Beside the window was a wardrobe, and the toilet alcove on the other side of the bed, which took up most of the floor space, was the size of the wardrobe.

On the pinkish fluffy bed cover lay a large portfolio, tied up with tapes, two of which had broken. The walls were papered with a yellowish wallpaper that was both bleak and friendly – like a vest which the room slept in and never took off.

At our age and with our past, it was normal that Sven and I had artist friends who had become successful, who were invited as guests of honour to Venice and stayed in the Hotel Danieli, and about whom monographs with many colour plates were written. They were good friends and when we met, we laughed a lot with them. We, however, each in his own fashion, were chronically unfashionable, or – to put it more baldly – we didn't sell much.

When together, Sven and I, we saw this as an honour, almost as part of a conspiracy. Not a conspiracy against us. God forbid. The conspiracy was ours: it was in our nature to resist, he in painting, I in writing. We weren't somewhere between success and failure, we were elsewhere.

A year or two ago, Sven began suffering from Parkinson's disease. When not holding a brush, his hand trembled considerably. I had ricked my back that summer bringing in hay and was suffering from sciatica.

So, there we were, two elderly men in rather crumpled clothes and with not very clean hands, edging our way crab-like along the narrow path around the bed in Room 19.

The lampshade on the fitted wall light which had only a 25-watt bulb in it was melon-coloured. Thirty years before at this time of year – the end of August – we used to walk through the melon fields of the Vaucluse, Sven with his paintbox and I with a camera, a Voejtlander. It's hot, his peasant friends would say to us, they quench the thirst, pick one whenever you want to.

He pulled back the window curtain to let in a little more light and air and I untied and opened the portfolio. In it was a pile of unstretched canvas which Sven had just painted in tempera. Open, the portfolio took up almost the whole double bed. I picked up a canvas and arranged it somehow to lean against the back of the chair at the foot of the bed. Sven remained standing. Then I went back to where the pillows were and sat down cautiously.

It's the left side, Sven asked, the sciatica?

Yes.

Is this the first? I asked him, nodding at the painting of sea and rocks.

No, it's one of the last; they're not in any order.

He had an unanxious but curious expression. Curious not, I believe, about my opinion, but about exactly what had happened when he painted the canvas.

Then we looked. It was very hot in the room and we were sweating, our shirts like the wallpaper. After a long while – but time had stopped – I got to my feet. Mind your back! Sven said. I went to examine more closely the canvas against the chair, then returned to the pillows and gazed.

What we were doing in Room 19, we had done several hundred times before in his studio, or on beaches, or outside the tent we slept in with our families, or against the windscreen of a Citroën 2CV or under cherry trees. And what we were doing was looking together intently, critically, silently, at something he had

167

brought back. I say *silently* but often on these occasions there was music in the air. The colours and lights and darks on the canvas and the traces of the stubby gestures of the brush – gestures which made it unmistakably a painting by Sven – made a kind of music. We could hear it now in the hotel bedroom.

Over the years piles of canvases, taken off their stretchers, had grown higher and higher in the lofts and basements of the houses through which he had passed. The pile on the bed was less than 5 centimetres high. The ones I'm thinking of were 2 metres high. Once finished, his paintings were discarded. Maybe they kept each other company in their piles.

Anyway there had never been time to bring them out and offer them to the world. There were a few exceptions – sometimes he gave a painting to a friend. Sometimes a maverick collector bought one. I remember a man who manufactured paints and lived in Marseille. All the other canvases were forgotten. And this seemed right because finally they belonged to the field or the oil tanker or the street of traffic or the dog which had been their starting point.

After forty years we both accepted this fatality which was also a happiness. When the canvases were put aside, they were carefree. No frames, no dealers, no museums, no literature, no worries. Only the very distant music.

Although we knew this, each time we examined a newly painted canvas we nevertheless did so with the critical concentration of judges selecting a painting for a permanent collection. We couldn't be bought and we couldn't be influenced.

The second canvas was on the chair. I got up to go closer.

Careful of your back! warned Sven.

Wet rocks seen from above.

I recognise something today which I didn't before. Sven is the last painter who looks at what is out there, as Cézanne and Pissarro did. He doesn't paint like them. He doesn't try to. But he *stands* there, brush in hand like them, his eyes open in the same way observing thoughtlessly. Thoughtlessly? Yes, following without asking why. This is what makes these men a little like saints and this is why their modesty is so unassumed.

The light from where the sun touched the wet rocks came through several layers of paint as if, impossibly, the light was the first thing painted.

We scrutinised canvas after canvas. We drank tepid mineral water as we sweated. Perhaps Room 19 of the Hotel du Printemps had never been filled with such an intensity of looking before. The unstretched canvases, with their ragged margins of white, carrying weeks of looking in Belle Île where they had been painted, and the two of us, studying each scribble of paint to ensure that nothing false should pass. And maybe this would still be true for Room 19 even if once or twice we were mistaken in our assessment.

Sven never sat down. Once he went into the toilet to splash some water on his face.

A canvas on which the pile of a green hill slid like the blade of a plough under a pale-orange sky at exactly the right angle to turn the landscape into a furrow.

I carry a spare egg with me always, Sven mused, in case I need to mix more colour.

[29]

Subcomandante
Insurgente

In a suburb to the south of Paris, France, a municipal swimming pool. In term-time the local schools use it and the indoor pool is only open to the public at certain hours. The public are serious women and men (of all ages) who swim up and down without a smile and wear black goggles to protect their eyes. Maybe swimming the length of the pool you pass one another fifty times but there's never a flicker of recognition. Single-minded fitness.

Now in July and August with the schools shut and the pool open to the public all day long, something changes. The place becomes a water playground for anybody who, for one reason or another, is not leaving the city for a holiday by the sea. (The reasons for not leaving are mostly economic.) Sisters come hand in hand, along with spinsters, truants, old-age pensioners and young fathers who teach their small children to swim. With its glass walls and tiled floors the whole place echoes with screams, laughter and the splashes of dare-devil dives.

People on beaches are usually indulgent to their bodies and so it's their bodies you notice; here it's not the bodies but the souls which grab your attention. The souls in bathing costumes. Some in the water, some climbing out, others about to jump in. Tight caps over the hair are obligatory – even for bald men. We have

hing else in common too – everybody here is
lay offering or learning a little confidence.

a bench outside, my towel drying in the sun, I
a book that has just been sent to me from New
.. It is a collection of letters and communiqués,
tten by Subcomandante Marcos between January
nd June of last year for the Zapatista Army of National
Liberation (EZLN). The story has been told across the
world many times.

Just after midnight (as usual we were late, Marcos
says in an aside), just after midnight on January the 1st
1994, an army of several thousand indigenous (Mayan)
men and women took up arms, seized the town of San
Cristobal in Chiapas, the poorest province of Mexico,
and challenged the federal government to recognise
their claims.

We are denied the most elementary education
so that they can use us as cannon fodder and
plunder our country's riches, uncaring that we are
dying of hunger and curable diseases. Nor do they
care that we have nothing, absolutely nothing, no
decent roof over our heads, no land, no work, no
health, no food, no education. We do not have the
right to freely and democratically elect our own
authorities, nor are we independent of foreigners,

174

nor do we have peace or justice for ourselves and our children. But today we say *Enough!*

After twelve days of fighting – during which the Mexican air force bombed villages which were thought to be pro-Zapatista – an uneasy cease-fire was agreed, which militarily speaking, gradually became a kind of stalemate. On one hand, the EZLN obliged to withdraw to the mountains but with a considerable part of the indigenous peasant population loyal to them and finding increasing support from civil society across the whole of Mexico; on the other hand, the federal army, with massively superior arms and numbers, and the private army of the ranchers hell-bent on destroying everything the Zapatistas stood for, but nervous and perplexed before the mountains which protect outlaws.

From these mountains in March the Subcomandante writes to a schoolboy who has sent him a photo of his dog:

I have the urge to write to you and tell you something about being 'the professionals of violence', as we have so often been called. Yes, we are professionals. But our profession is hope ... out of our spent and broken bodies must rise up a new world . . . Will we see it? Does it matter? I believe that it doesn't matter as much as knowing with undeniable certainty that it will be born, and that we have put our all – our lives, bodies and souls – into this long and painful but historic birth. *Amor y dolor* – love and pain: two words that not only rhyme, but join up and march together.

A kid comes out of the municipal swimming pool with his feet in the air and walks down the steps on his hands, laughing. Clowns go on. In French public life, however, humour has practically disappeared, for there is not enough energy left to spare for it. Tired public men! Surprisingly, in the mountains the Subcomandante still has that energy and in the book on my lap there's a joke on every other page.

The style has of course become legendary, but don't let us be confused by the word style. True style is inseparable from what is being said, it's not something chosen. And in my own experience as a writer it's also inseparable from the voices I'm listening to when trying to write. The style in question here combines modesty with unflinching excess:

Don't forget what our path was. We sincerely looked for other doors that might open to admit our timid light. You must now learn from this sad story. Never forget the words that made us important, although it was only for a moment: *everything for everyone, nothing for ourselves.*

The excess is not that of political extremism. The Zapatistas have no political programme to impose; they have a political conscience which they hope will spread through their example. The excess comes from their conviction (which personally I accept completely) that they also represent the dead, all the maltreated dead – the dead who are less forgotten in Mexico than anywhere else in the world. No mystics, they believe in words being handed down through the suffering and the centuries, and they hate lies:

Here we are, the forever dead, dying once again, but now in order to live.

Twenty months after the insurrection, the outcome in Chiapas is uncertain. The Zapatistas, still armed, have recently called for a national and international popular Convention to come together to consider their demands.

The Mexican economy, hailed by the IMF last year as a world model of contemporary development, collapsed last winter and was only saved by international capital for fear of a world crisis. In exchange for the largest loan (50 billion dollars) ever accorded to a country, the Mexican government put their petrol in hock for ever and agreed to step up the neo-liberal economic shock treatment they have been applying for the last thirteen years – half the active population is under-employed.

The Mexicans were also told – notably by the Chase Manhattan Bank – to eliminate the Zapatistas who were bad for the confidence of foreign investors. 'The moment has come,' announced *Fortune* magazine six months ago in New York, 'to buy Mexico!'

Meanwhile, thanks to newspapers, particularly in Mexico and Spain, and thanks to Internet which no government has yet found a way of policing, the Zapatista Declarations are being more and more eagerly read across the world and their stand appreciated and supported. Their message is reaching Santiago, Berlin, Barcelona, even the suburbs of Paris.

A strange unprecedented ideological struggle between a few thousand faceless but true men and women, hidden in the sheltering mountains, and the triumphant World Order. How is such an unequal duel possible, if 'only for a moment'?

Everywhere these days more and more people knock their heads against the fact that the future of our planet and what it will offer or deny to its inhabitants, is being decided by boards of men who control more money than all the governments in the world, who never stand for election, and whose sole criterion for every decision they take is whether or not it increases or is prone to increase Profit.

No one except those men and their ideological pupils really believes, after the evidence of the last five years, in the promises of the Free Market triumphant. Deep down people know, when they wake up at 4 a.m., that, one day, the system is going to crack. At dawn they bow their heads once again and obediently try not to go under. But the doubts are beginning. And at 4 a.m. the Subcomandante talks to us.

I get up from the bench and walk along the street in the shade under the plane trees. I pass nobody. The first leaves are falling. At the corner I go into a small shop to buy groceries. A man with a beard wearing shorts, a little younger than I, is mumbling to the shopkeeper who is a Lebanese. I gather that the shopkeeper has given him a large paper bag of black bananas because they are far too overripe to sell. Now the man is slowly counting out coins to pay for a tin. A large tin of meat for dogs. His hands tell me unequivocally that he is homeless.

The Subcomandante explains why he is addicted to postscripts:

> It happens that one feels that something has remained between the fingers, that there are still some words that want to find their way into sentences, that one has not finished emptying the pockets of the soul. But it is useless, there never will be a postscript that can contain so many nightmares . . . and so many dreams.